Metaphorosis

January 2021

Beautifully made speculative fiction

Also from Metaphorosis

Verdage

Reading 5X5 x2: Duets
Score – an SFF symphony
Reading 5X5: Readers' Edition
Reading 5X5: Writers' Edition

Metaphorosis Magazine

Metaphorosis: Best of 20xx
Metaphorosis 20xx: The Complete Stories
annual issues, from 2016

Monthly issues

Plant Based Press

Best Vegan Science Fiction & Fantasy
annual issues, from 2016

from B. Morris Allen:
Susurrus
Allenthology: Volume I
Tocsin: and other stories
Start with Stones: collected stories
Metaphorosis: a collection of stories

Metaphorosis

January 2021

---

edited by
B. Morris Allen

ISSN: 2573-136X (online)
ISBN: 978-1-64076-191-9 (e-book)
ISBN: 978-1-64076-192-6 (paperback)

Metaphorosis
a magazine of speculative fiction

from
Metaphorosis Publishing

Neskowin

January 2021

Superbloom

Lynne Peskoe-Yang

The call comes in the evening, though it's morning on the other side of the world. K. is demanding that I leave my study right this minute to look at the sea. I grab my sample bag and rush outside, too curious to argue. It takes less than a minute for me to jog from my house to the end of the jetty.

I peer down at the surface of the water. I can't see much; the sun set ten minutes ago.

"What am I looking for?"

"Look at the water. What color is it?"

I fumble in my bag for my good flashlight—one I made myself, with a patented triple lens—and turn its ultra-sharp beam on the ocean.

"Why is it doing that?" I whisper. "Why is it just sitting still?"

"What color is it, D.?"

"Green. The whole thing is just solid green."

A long, textured sigh issues from my earpiece. "God," K. hisses. She seems on the verge of tears, but with some effort she controls her breathing.

I can't wait. "Is this that algae bloom of yours? What the hell is it doing here?"

She inhales purposefully. I hoped she'd have to pull herself together to correct me, and it works; when she speaks again, her voice is steady.

"Not algae. It's a lichen—or it was when I started studying it. I've got no idea what it's doing there, other than growing. I'm still making sense of it myself. Do you remember my dissertation?"

Of course I remember. A year ago, K. printed out that dissertation and mailed it to me personally, neatly stapled and, I thought, perfumed. I read the abstract a dozen times before I gave in and called. She explained it all to me, in her laughing-brook voice, with a patience I hadn't been shown since I was a girl.

She had found me in a directory of remote researchers and wrote to ask me to photograph some of the lichens in my little biome, which was, she pointed out meaningfully, on the exact opposite side of the world from where K. herself lived, in New Zealand.

In the dissertation K. had referred to the floating, living islands that popped up along the northwestern coast as "ur-lichens", or, in more casual contexts, "super-lichens".

It was the second name that caught on in her small collective of Māori ecologists, the only ones paying attention at first. The super-lichen was a local disaster, overshadowed by the death rattle of the oceanic coral reefs. The collective relied on a growing network of citizen scientists to track the expansion—what they came to call the Bloom—as it spread unchecked along the coastline.

K. had volunteered to make contact with someone who could keep the last watch, as far away from the origin as possible. My island outpost, her own antipode, would mark the finish line for a fully global superbloom, if it ever got that far. I didn't ask her what good it would do anyone to know how much of the ocean was lost at that point. I don't think either of us expected that such a thing could actually happen in our lifetimes.

When the Bloom began to move down the northwestern coast of New Zealand, K. packed up her belongings and moved with it. She still called me occasionally to ask for updates from my side of the world. I would take the call on my headset while I worked the glass.

"A fungal spore sends its hyphae into the algae," she'd say, drawing out the Greek ending—*hy-fee*—in a grin that I could almost see. Through my headset I could hear her, even while I sanded finished prisms or made coke fuel for the forge. Sometimes she asked me about my work, but I had no talent for translation.

Instead, I sent photos, both of the growing lens and the lichens—no samples, she said, as the risk of contamination was overwhelming. I also sent her tools. Funding was scarce for lichen-watching, but I had all the raw materials at my disposal to replicate and improve every piece of glassware K. needed, and shockproof shipping was free under my contract. When K.'s digital microscope was stolen, I sent her a replacement—a bespoke mechanical version from my own workshop, with a hardwood carrying case, hand-engraved with her initials.

After that, the calls were daily. My ears adapted to the sound of K.'s voice and listened for it even after we hung up. I could not help but absorb her passion, her creeping panic, over the terrible might of the Bloom. Alone of ocean beings, it seemed to delight in the spiking acidity caused by human pollution. The Bloom was so good at growing, so blazingly energy-efficient, especially near the surface, that huge mats of it emerged in shallow waters around dozens of islands in the South Pacific. Where they met the coasts, the floating mats merged, surrounding whole archipelagos in swamps that turned alarmingly toxic.

I asked K. how it reproduced.

"This one doesn't," she said. "It only grows."

This is what I learned in those months of building: a lichen is not an organism, but a community of organisms acting collectively. The photosynthetic members, single algae cells or long strands of sun-loving cyanobacteria, feed the fungus via the hyphae, which penetrate the algae's cell walls to extract their sugars. In return, the fungus offers a safe habitat for its support organisms. Together, the hyphae and the photosynthetic cells make a single continuous unit of life, self-replicating and infinitely adaptable.

"On its own, the fungus is a clump of hyphae. It can't form any discernible structures. It dies."

"So the fungus is a parasite?"

"We'd have to ask the algae."

We passed good months this way, her calling, me listening. She was my favorite sound.

Then the Superbloom took the rest of the ocean in the course of a single night, twenty years ahead of schedule, and K. called me again.

"When I woke up this morning, I thought my satellite feed was broken—the map was just covered." It's hard to process her words.

"…But if it's reached you already, we're long past any way of stopping the spread," she concluded.

I listen to the birdsong through the phone: a kookaburra's alien laughter. Behind it, the wind is high, as it is here. I can see the first storm of summer growing on the horizon.

The kookaburra falls silent. I wipe my eyes with my forearm.

"Is there anything we can do? Maybe if...?" I trail off, unable to even frame the question.

"You should stock some food," she says gently. "If I think of something, I'll... I'll let you know."

It's fully dark now. The vast, pale expanse could almost be the natural ocean, if it weren't for the disturbing stillness of it beneath the starless sky. I feel panic rise, tightening my lungs and heart.

"Oh, and D.? Are you still there?"

I cough, force my voice deeper. "Yeah."

"Don't touch it."

The Caldera is the perfect place to light a beacon, and I was once the perfect person to keep it lit. My technical training is in photonics, the art of manipulating and redirecting light. I was one of the first to build lenses from gadolinite, the oily black mineral that makes up the base of the Caldera, though I did it in the comfort of my childhood home on the mainland. But I was losing patience with the frantic pace of manufacturing; I was ready for a quieter life.

By then, I had made some friends in government, and one of them shared my name with the Bureau of Scientific Engagement, a collaboration between government scientists and propagandists. Riding a wave of investment in space ventures, the project aimed to thrill the nation by building a self-powering radio beacon that would send an eternal message to alien worlds. Previous communications to the extrasolar expanse had been ephemeral: a five-minute transmission from the North Pole of spoken greetings in two hundred Earth languages; a gold disk embossed with Da Vinci's naked eight-limbed man and some other things, launched into the sky. The time had come, in the BSE's opinion, to make ourselves known to the universe on a permanent basis.

A simple transmitter would emit a continuous wavelength: a hundred mHz, just energetic enough to escape the atmosphere. My job would be to build and then maintain a lens out of gadolinite thermal glass, a form of passive solar power. The lens would both concentrate the signal into a narrow beam and power itself virtually forever, storing solar energy in a solid-state battery that fed the same monotone signal, even at night.

I was to build the whole thing on-site, on a colonial outpost with no other lucrative resources to offer, nor remaining residents to exploit. The Caldera is an empty-named place, a safe enough distance from real human civilization that the mainland, at least, would have warning, should the worst occur. What the worst might entail, we did not discuss.

The day after the Superbloom starts the same as usual, and it's not until I look out the window that I recall what has changed. The Caldera is a narrow island, curled like a fetus against the sea. To my left, the bulk of the island, a great crescent of steaming jungle, pours down into the bay as always. But the basin itself is deathly still, suffocating under the weight of a mat of new life that extends, waveless, to every horizon.

It's hard to look at.

Above the Bloom, on top of the hills on the opposite end of the crescent island, the black, flat-topped needle of the signal tower is barely visible from here. It's been three months since I got it running, and two months since I hauled my personal items to the opposite side of the island from the tower, into one of the last remaining buildings on the island. The tower was starting to make my head buzz.

I check the monitor: the signal is fine. A one-note performance, without even the texture of an ending, communicating the bare minimum of reality. The beam moves like an out-of-control spotlight, the focused radio waves sweeping around the planet as it turns, carving out curly ribbons of space in their near-random search for a receptive target. In the early days of the project, there had been some talk of sending out a message with actual content, even a simple greeting. But then one of our physicists showed that if we stuck to one frequency, the signal could easily reach the nearest galaxy cluster and would likely be detectable at twice that distance. The programming team was furious, but *intergalactic* sounded better than *interplanetary* in the headlines, so the one-note message won out.

My contract gives me a year of watch after I finish construction, but already it is impossible to picture life on the mainland. No word has arrived from my supervisors, but that doesn't surprise me. Will I last nine more months here, without supplies, without a plan? I do not dwell on this.

That night, I make my first discovery.

"The Bloom emits light." My words echo on the other end. Does my voice sound different to her because she's listening to its inverted form—across the world, upside down, in broad daylight?

"I thought I was seeing things," she whispers after a moment.

"I see it, too. It's clearer at night, but even in the light it's pulsing. Why?"

"I don't know." Her voice is hushed, hurried, as though someone might be listening. "It wasn't doing this even a week ago, but this Bloom changes so fast. If it were to somehow recruit some new microorganism, something that glows..."

"A third colony member?"

"It's possible. We wouldn't know. But there are hundreds of bioluminescent species."

"Why do they glow?"

"Camouflage. Prey attraction. Signaling to the predators that eat *their* predators."

"Would that look like... a pulse? Rhythmic?"

"No. It's purely responsive."

"Doesn't the pulse remind you of a heartbeat?"

"Yes, of course."

In the green expanse of the bay, a field of little leaflets drinks in the dimmed sun. On the far side, straight across the bay, the black crown of the signal tower looms like a purposeless alien.

"Does the Bloom, or some part of it, *have* a heartbeat?"

"Absolutely not."

Later, a call from the department: deliveries will be suspended for the time being, given the circumstances. I do not have to ask what the circumstances are. All around the world, I imagine, human beings are attempting to negotiate with the invader, touching and hacking and plowing, growing more desperate for a response. But the Bloom will not hear them, any more than I would hear a threat spelled out in plant hormones.

I tell him I have enough food for a few months and not to worry about me. There is shouting in the background, but I can't make out the words; the call ends, thankfully, before I get invested. I am sensing already that I shouldn't spend my panic on people I already know. It is easy to forget them; what could I do for them from here?

The sky is sickly green in the evening when the light begins to pulse again.

One-two. It is unmistakably a heartbeat, reborn as two flashes of incandescent plant-flesh, and yet no part of the Bloom could possibly have even a vestigial memory of having a heart. I count eighty beats per minute: a healthy resting heart rate for a human.

One-two. The rate does not change. If it's a message, it is insultingly simple. There is no hint of frustration, no pleading, no aggression; just a double-tap of light, repeating endlessly. A beacon reporting back that conditions are normal, stand by. *One-two.* A binary code too flat to be called communication. In Morse code, I recall uselessly, it is just the capital letter *I*, over and over and over, stupidly iterating into the dark.

I am here. Are you?

I creep to the edge of the Bloom. From the jetty, I drop a rock into its depths, as I often did when the ocean was still liquid, and watch the surface roll away from the impact in a stunted parody of wave motion. If I close my eyes while doing this and pay attention only to the splash, I will remember that there is still water under there.

I squat, scooping a handful of black sand from the beach and letting it pour from my fingers onto the curling leaves of the colony. No ripple at all. The living matter absorbs the motion, stunts its impact, so it can't be transferred. The motion is born locally, dies locally; sound, spoken prayer, would be stifled the same way.

But the Bloom *is* connected to itself, somehow. The pulse of the lichen at my feet is perfectly in phase with the pulse at the horizon. Light, then, can cross the channels from one end of the Bloom to the other. The Bloom is not a creature, but a culture; light is its language.

I don't know any words in light, but I don't think that would matter, if I could make some kind of deliberate pattern. The intent to speak is its own kind of speech— the astrobiologists taught me that. As long as the signal is clearly *meant* as a message, it is one.

"Fine," says K. when she calls back, too early. She woke me up. "Fine. It's sentient."

"I told you. There's no other explanation."

"Hm." I can hear her pacing. "Yes. But that doesn't mean—"

"Why are you so worried? This is a good thing. Maybe we can reason with it."

"Not good. Unprecedented. Bizarre. I can't even philosophically wrap my head around it. The pattern makes intelligent life unmistakable. Why would a living being advertise its existence like that? What takes that kind of stupid risk?"

"You're the one who's studied it. What do you think?"

She exhales. I can hear her brain working. "I think... whatever it is, it doesn't know we're here. Yet. But it's looking."

"I'm going to answer."

"With the beacon? Is it moveable? I thought you couldn't redirect the beam."

"I can do it. I just never had to before."

"Okay. Okay. But D., listen. This is not a conversation with a person. Sentience is not the same thing as a brain. I've been studying this thing. It evolves faster than its components, faster even than some viruses, but it also started pulsing all at once, like a single organism... If this is intelligence, it's clearly distributed— spread out in the body of the Bloom, coordinated, but not centralized. It is *nothing* like us."

"What is it like?"

"God. Fuck. I don't know. An octopus?" She's close to tears. "Who knows what it would do if it recognized another intelligence? And you want to give away your position, before we even know what will happen! What if it takes the signal as a threat? What if it *answers*?"

Her voice is so plaintive, so childish, that I half want to shout at her. *There is no other option!* But I can't say that. She knows.

For a moment I consider telling her I was planning to come see her when my contract was up, but even thinking the words makes me want to howl.

Instead, I tell K. I love her, and then I hang up in a hurry so I don't have to hear her sob.

In the evening, I trek north. I weave among my discarded shipping containers, most twice my height, their steel now coated in the rich green of a kudzu infestation at least a foot deep on every face. The vines are flowering on the southeast side where I approach; I breathe in clouds of grape-like perfume as I pass each cluster of white and purple blossoms.

The place steams with life. Between the blocks and everywhere the vines haven't claimed lies a thick carpet of mosses in varying shades, from pine-green to chartreuse and golden yellow. Already, beneath my boots, the fragile stalks of a bryophyte have been crushed into wet salad.

I need my flashlight to find the ladder on the far side of the tower. I hover on the bottom rung, waiting for the doubts to come; but my wonderful brain is silent, and I hear nothing but the wind through the leaves. The top rung is covered in seagull scat, so I have to haul myself onto the platform beneath the beacon like a sea lion. I turn off my light and recover there for a few moments, with my back against the thin railing, staring upward.

The sky is clear now. The compound lens of the beacon looms over me, its outer rings glittering with reflected stars. The pieces are arranged in concentric circles, like a slice of a giant black onion. Each layer is made of two to thirty segments of gadolinite glass.

It is impossible to tell by sight that the signal is firing. I pass my hand over the opening in the center of the onion slice, and imagine that I can feel it, a sort of metaphysical buzz; but I know I can't actually feel anything, as surely as I know the signal exists. The beam, even concentrated by my lens, is both silent and invisible to me.

I pull myself up with a groan and stretch upward to run my hands along one of the rings. The dark glass is warmer than I remembered. The smaller rings are closely nested and hard to differentiate by starlight, so I work my way inward by feel. Just below the innermost ring, attached to the pole that supports the beacon's weight, there is a latched metal box, unlocked.

The terminal inside is still charged. I power it up and it chirps softly, as though it recognizes me. Black letters appear against the green-grey field: I N P U T ?

My mind is empty. I turn away from the beacon and nearly lose my balance. The railing, rusted from the salt spray, groans but holds steady for now. How is it up to *me* to decide what to say to an alien from my own planet?

It has stopped glowing, I realize as I stare into the sea, so it's possible I've missed my chance, but somehow, inexplicably, I feel that it is actually aware of what I am doing and has simply paused to wait for my answer. *Impossible!* I can almost hear K. say in response.

I picture her on the other side of the world and feel my spine straighten a bit.

I take great, gulping breaths of the briny air. I reprogram the beacon.

I fiddle with latches in the dark. The lens is twice my wingspan and half my weight, but at least the whole thing comes off its mount without so much as a screwdriver. I hoist it onto my shoulder like a parasol and then lower the circular end to the platform, feeling my long trek across the island screaming in my kneecaps. When I stand up, the beam is pointing just below the horizon, its waves colliding with a distant section of the Bloom's vast body.

The Bloom is still as stone. In the silvery light, the world looks primordial, as though made of just-cooled magma, unmarred by soil or water. But I know the Bloom is there and watching me, in its own way; it holds its breath as I hold mine.

We watch each other.

Just where the beam hits, a part of the Bloom begins to rise. But this is an illusion: it is simply luminescing, first there and then all over, the whole field of it suddenly turning white with light—far brighter than before. In seconds I'm forced to cover my eyes with my arm, but it's not enough.

I wake up on the beach a few meters from the tower, my whole body aching from the fall. The world is still flashing around me, so bright I can almost hear the new pattern: the same one I chose moments or hours ago.

Long, short, long. *K*, the Bloom is saying, shouting, singing, to me and to her, and I can feel her amazement radiating straight through the center of the Earth.

See Lynne Peskoe-Yang's story "Superbloom" online at Metaphorosis.
If you liked it, leave a comment. Authors love that!
Remember to subscribe to our e-mail updates so you'll know when new stories are posted.

About the story

I wrote this in an attempt to relate to a kind of organism I find unfathomable. I think I'm jealous of lichen, the way it smoothly integrates two distinct sets of DNA into a single body, without conflict or suspicion. I wanted to fuse with something like that, so I wrote about someone who I thought would understand that impulse.

A question for the author

Q: What are you currently reading?

A: *Uzumaki*, the graphic horror novel by Junji Ito.

About the author

Lynne Peskoe-Yang is a science fiction writer and tech journalist living in the Northeast US.

lynnepeskoeyang.com, @lynnepeskoeyang

All We Ever Look For

Cécile Cristofari

When I opened the window this morning, three parrots were perched in a tree hanging over a deserted beach of pure white sand that stretched towards a dazzling horizon. I'd never seen anything so lovely. I leaned out, just enough to feel the caress of the breeze, the salty coolness of the surf that helped me brace myself for the day ahead. Not long after closing the window, I opened the front door with a deep breath, stepping into the rumble of traffic and the dappled shadow of a maple, in the damp heat of Québec summer.

The memory of that shore and gentle seaside wind stayed with me for the entire bus ride. It was gone now, I knew. What happened when I closed my window I could only guess; the wonders it let me glimpse vanished as soon as the latch clicked shut, and never came back. Now, watching my own world scroll past the bus, I wished I had left my window open a little longer.

When I reached the office, the two secretaries were talking about the latest missing person cases in town. I stared at them for longer than I should have. They waved, a little awkwardly.

My desk was in a corner of the office, out of sight, just under a mercifully powerful fan. I wiped my brow, and exchanged perfunctory greetings with my neighbours. I had never been good at making friends at the office. Neither was I cut out for the increasingly heavy heat waves these days, it seemed, and I had another fleeting thought of how lovely and cool that beach had seemed.

From across the office, Marie-Ange interrupted my train of thought with a wave and a conspiratorial gesture, placing a folded bit of paper on the corner of her desk. I answered with an uncertain smile.

The heat had not abated when I returned home. I still held Marie-Ange's crumpled note in my fist. *Saturday?* it simply read. I had waited for her break to leave the office so I wouldn't have to respond.

I wondered if this was what guilt felt like.

I sat, or rather dropped, in the armchair facing the window, to scratch Toutou's ears as Tilou mewed in protest at being woken up. I stared at the maple billowing outside—when the window was closed it never showed anything but the maple outside the building, its branches stretched far and wide like a challenge to the concrete and cars and heat and fires and everything humans could throw at its kind. It was only when I opened it that the magic began.

I had never figured out how or why this treasure had fallen into my hands. I never heard reports of other portals opening elsewhere in the world, and the question of what I had done to deserve this one was never answered. One day I'd opened the window in my living room, hoping to get some fresh air while I read the news as usual with a cat peering over my shoulder —and instead of the customary drone of the street, I'd gazed over a cliff, snow-capped mountains dotting the horizon under an uncanny white sky. I'd banged the window shut in shock, only to open it again, seconds later. This time it was a desert, red sands stretching as far as I could see. The dance had begun then, opening and closing, never knowing what strangeness would lie beyond, only that it would be new, and odd, and marvellous— and that as soon as I closed the window, it would disappear forever.

At first I had sworn to myself that I would never let anyone else see it, but soon that had felt petty, and I'd begun to bring people in. The first few times, it had been simple, even made me a little proud for the first time in years. An act of sharing and compassion, inviting unhappy acquaintances to sit with me and gaze at the wonders beyond my window before walking back home with a lighter heart. They must have thought it was nothing more than a clever display; so had I, at first, and so did most people until the very last second. The truth was too extraordinary to entertain.

The first time someone asked to step through, I had only gaped. The possibility of it had never occurred to me. Her name was Angélique, I recall, and she was a widow, just about my age, with an estranged son. Two days after I'd agreed to her request (it hadn't occurred to me that I might do otherwise), I'd watched her step over the window ledge and on the grassy slope of a mountain meadow. She'd secured her backpack and blown me a kiss, and only when the window pane clicked shut had I fully realised that the door to her world was now gone, and she would never be able to come out again.

After Angélique, there were others. I had a knack for light friendships, the seemingly shallow ones, acquaintances that would not disturb the quiet of my home. They almost always started in the same way: an exchange of glances on the bus or a café, a smile, a few minutes of conversation that usually led to a farewell, after a moment of companionship I'd enjoy but wouldn't miss. And then sometimes the conversation lasted longer, until I sensed that sadness, that longing I'd come to know so well, until I realised that I held the key to the one thing these people wanted.

It had been easy at first, watching them step through and waving farewell, sometimes wiping a little tear, telling myself I'd brought someone more happiness than anyone else ever could have. I only had to pretend that these people were just like me, lonely and stranded, with no one to miss them. It was only when the first missing person reports came up in the newspaper that I had to face the facts. There are many ways to be lonely, and not all of them are irreparable.

"How did you pick such a silly auntie?" I asked Tilou out loud. She rubbed her head against my cheek.

I petted her and stared ahead until, as always happened after sitting alone with my thoughts for too long, I felt compelled to get up. After some hesitation, I opened the window.

Outside, a deep rainforest was alive with whistles and fluted sounds, the songs of birds and beasts I had no name for. I leaned out and closed my eyes as the mist from a waterfall cooled my face, spraying scents of moss and orchids. My smile slowly returned, and for a very long time I stood there, trying to catch the sight of monkeys or tree frogs behind every rustling leaf.

My cats, the only companions I had, would be just as happy with any other owner, I suddenly thought. I would miss them for a while, but it would be nothing to make sure they spent the rest of their lives in a home that would be just as good as mine. There was nothing holding me here. The notion was unexpectedly comforting. My life was my own. Whatever I chose to do with it, however foolhardy, I would not hurt anyone else. One day, I decided, I would go too. But today was not the right time; I was out of cat food, and anyway, I was already too weary of the summer heat to enjoy a rainforest for long.

As always, eventually, I closed the window, and I could hear once again the endless drone of the cars in the street, as clouds gathered overhead for the evening storm.

Wednesday morning sailed by in its customary haze of boredom, until a shadow loomed at the edge of my desk.

"Got time for a sandwich?"

I jumped, startled from yet another reverie. Marie-Ange was standing in front of me, her bag already slung over her shoulder. "Come on. The falafel ones. You know you love those."

My eyes darted around my desk for an excuse not to go out. The blank file staring at me from the computer screen was enough of an answer. The prospect of going out was not that unappealing, come to think of it. I got up, groaned when my back protested, and stayed in place just long enough for Marie-Ange to drag me by the arm, waving to everybody that was left in the office.

The space outside the building was not a particularly scenic one: a large car park with a few maples and a couple of grassy banks on the side, where we sat in what shade we could find. Marie-Ange finished her salad in a couple of bites, then sprawled in the grass on her back, grinning.

"Look at how gorgeous that tree is," she said.

I smiled. In truth, it wasn't much of a tree, just a sapling they'd replanted as a token gesture after they'd razed the field to make way for cars. But Marie-Ange's enthusiasm never deserted her. No one else would have convinced me, for the third time this week, to take a break and breathe the outside air when I could instead have got rid of my work and ridden back home half an hour earlier. It still surprised me, sometimes, that she not only talked me into it, but made me *want* to do it. Now that I looked at the sunlight splintering through the maple leaves, I, too, began to see some beauty in that gracile, tenacious little tree.

Marie-Ange propped herself up on her elbow.

"So. About Saturday."

My heart sank at once.

"Saturday?"

"You promised you'd show me. Remember?"

I did, very well. It had happened at the start of summer, on a day when Marie-Ange had decided to drag me out of the city for ice cream after work. I'd grumbled and wondered why she would bother with me. But as we drove across the bridge to Orleans Island, she'd pointed to the waterfall on the other side of the channel, and started gushing in the way she sometimes did about the most mundane little things, and I'd felt something unexpected—a flicker of girlish delight, the simple pleasure of feeling the damp heat on my face and the smells of the blooming forest stretching in front of us. It was a long time since I'd felt that way outside of my living room. And then I'd felt something even stronger: gratitude, pure joy at being with someone who would so casually offer this sense of wonder to me.

I'd wanted to offer something else in return. I had told her about the one thing I'd ever had that mattered. And now I wished I hadn't.

"All right,' I muttered. 'Just one look. Don't tell anyone about it, okay?"

She agreed, still grinning. It was time to go back to work. On the way back in, she changed the subject, and my mood lightened. If she thought I was only going to show her an amusing trick, so much the better.

On the bus ride back home, someone was reading the headlines out loud, and the lady behind her burst into tears. Her friend comforted her, saying something about the uplifting notes all these people had left, that they couldn't have been taken by force or ended up in a bad place. I swallowed and moved to the back of the bus.

Québec City officials overwhelmed by missing persons epidemic, I read on my phone later in the night. Three more in a month. A secret cult, underground experiments, theories were blooming all over the place. I shoved the device back in my pocket.

Missing persons epidemic, indeed, I thought to myself, as if facing a crowd of haunted relatives demanding justice. *What if I told you that they wanted to go? That they made this decision by themselves, knowing fully well what it would do to you? Would you blame* me?

I stopped as I realised that I was starting to mouth the words out loud. From their place on the sofa, Toutou and Tilou were gazing at me, green eyes and yellow eyes indolently blinking in a pool of sunlight. I had been living on my own for too long.

I leaned out of the window one last time before going to bed, to breathe in the smell of salty wind. Tilou had jumped off the sofa, and with a soft thud, landed herself on the sill; she didn't complain when I gently picked her off and held her against my chest so she could watch safely. A marble balcony hung over a rocky coast with pines and aloes tumbling into the sea. Underneath, the waters shimmered, light and deep blue interlocking towards the horizon. A fish leapt up below me, sending a flash of silver over the water. When a seagull dove, missed, and flew back up with a cry of frustration, Tilou tensed, and at last wriggled free and strolled back to the sofa, all interest in other universes gone. I watched the bird until it disappeared over a clump of dark green trees, knowing that I could follow it if I wanted to. I thought once more of all those who had gone through, of the felicity they had seized for themselves, the mourning they had left behind.

Then I thought of Marie-Ange. It had been an imprudent idea to invite her. But it would turn out fine, I hoped. She would understand that this absolutely needed to remain a secret. And she would only take a look. She, at least, was perfectly happy with the world she lived in. Perhaps she could even come back, I mused, and we could stand in front of the window together, bet on what we would see that day, count to three, open it...

Maybe that was what friendship felt like. I smiled, closed the window, and went to bed next to a comfortably snoring cat.

On Friday, Marie-Ange dragged me out for lunch again. We chatted (or she did, while I smiled and nodded) all through the way to the fast food joint. When we sat down in the grass, however, her expression suddenly changed.

"I'm going to ask you something really outlandish. You can laugh at me if you want, but promise me you'll tell me the truth. All right?"

There was nothing I could do but swallow my dismay and acquiesce.

"I saw those missing persons reports on the news," she went on. "This is absurd. Québec City is as safe as it's always been. These... other worlds you said your window opened to. People haven't actually *gone in* there, have they?"

"Please don't tell anyone," I blurted out.

She opened her mouth. Covered it with her hand. For a few moments, she seemed halfway between laughter and tears, long enough for me to hope that it would be the former. I could handle being dismissed as a cat lady with one too many quirks. But if she started to accuse, threatened to denounce me...

"I need to see it," she said.

I breathed deeply.

"Yes. Of course. Just see it. Swear to me you won't tell anyone?"

"Not a chance. Don't worry."

"Thank you.' I realised that I held my hands balled tight against my stomach. I unclenched them and spread them on my knees. 'These people wanted to go, you know. It's not a decision they rushed into. I wouldn't have let them if they hadn't wanted it so badly."

"I know."

"I suppose it can't look good when you read the papers. But it won't happen again. I've been thinking about it lately. I'm going to quit. The only ones who knew about my portal are gone, and I'll keep it to myself now. And you, of course. Nobody's going to disappear again."

Marie-Ange made a strange face and touched my arm.

"I want to go," she said.

That evening, for the first time, I opened my living-room window with no anticipatory thrill, only through the force of habit.

Through the entire day, Marie-Ange's words had bounced around in my head, as if trapped in a vertiginous echo chamber—*I want to go*—along with my next, foolish question—*Why?* —as if asking her to explain herself would make her realise that there was no good reason for such a wish after all. Her explanations, however, had left me no space to argue.

The world was too small a place, more so with every passing day. I'd admired her ability to light up at every little joy life could throw her way, so much that I hadn't noticed how tired she was that small blessings were all our world had to offer her.

Or perhaps I simply was incapable of imagining how she felt. I could not recall the last time I had felt genuine delight outside of my living-room. How the person who had communicated that wonder to me could be unsatisfied with the world she lived in was unfathomable.

My thoughts ebbed as the landscape before me came into focus. Pillars of crystal in a translucent sea reflected the light of the setting sun into my living room. I stood there for long minutes, unable to take my eyes off the twin moons overhead.

How could the universe have decided that I would be the best person to entrust this portal to, of all the places it could have appeared? There was no answer but the gentle song of the water, lapping, flowing towards a horizon that seemed to curve more sharply than the one at the end of an earthly sea. I rested my hand on the sill. If I leaned out, only a little, perhaps I could touch the closest pillar. What would greet me out there—the thin air and cold of a mountain pass, or inviting warmth like the tropics at the dawn of time? I stood on tiptoe, reached forward. The breeze of another world stroked my fingers, like a hand, urging me forward with infinite gentleness. If I left now, there would be no more guilt, no more worry. One step out was all it would take...

I pulled my arm, closed the window, my heart beating faster than it should have. Tomorrow, I would call Marie-Ange and tell her I couldn't let her through. She would understand, I was certain of it. And then I'd never open that window again.

I came home late the next day, exhausted by my Saturday chores and the constant drone of the city, but with renewed resolve to make the phone call I needed to end this.

The day had slipped by so frantically I'd forgotten to check the time.

As soon as I took out my phone, the bell rang. When I opened, a flustered Marie-Ange dropped her huge backpack on my feet. After a second of shock, I swore at myself in silence. As usual, I had let time carry me along, not taking action until the last moment.

I made her sit down and have a glass of water.

"I drank on my way. Can I go now?" she said. Then with a nervous giggle, "If I don't I'm going to have second thoughts!"

I pushed the glass in front of her.

"We're not doing this, Marie-Ange," I blurted out.

She opened her eyes wide. My voice shook, but for once I could find the words, and didn't let her speak.

"Maybe it sounds like this is what you need, but it's wrong. I can't keep this up. You'll end up who knows where, in a parallel universe where you could die tomorrow, and no one would ever know. Ever. My window has never opened twice on the same place. Your family will be shattered, and if I meet them face to face,

I won't even be able to tell them you're all right. Because I won't know that. I'm sorry. And your family won't be the only ones. I…"

The cascading words dried up then. How I felt about her departure was my own concern. I couldn't expect her to alter her decision on my account, shouldn't even think of asking. I stood, silent, expecting her to make a fuss. But she nodded as if she understood.

"No matter what I tell them, people will be upset," she said. "They'll have to understand. This is what I need."

"Why?"

But I realised that I knew already. Loneliness was not the only force that drove people to seek what lay beyond my window. Her yearning for a new world matched my own, almost exactly. She only had one thing I lacked: enough courage to plunge into the unknown, while I remained trapped here, between marvellous worlds I would never know and one I still had to figure out.

Out of kindness, perhaps, Marie-Ange only smiled, and if she had guessed what I was thinking, she kept it quiet.

"Can I ask you something?" she said as if I hadn't spoken.

I leaned back. Not everyone asked *that* question, but I'd got it often enough, with varying degrees of awe, condescension or repulsion. Marie-Ange merely sounded curious.

"Why do this so far? Why help so many people?"

"*Help* truly isn't the word you want," I replied.

Thoughts of the weeping lady on the bus—someone's mother? Or friend? I'd never know—came unbidden. It had felt like the right thing to do, at the time. Yet all I could witness now was people hurting; I would never know how the people I had 'helped' had fared, nor even if they were still alive.

"It seemed wrong to have a magic portal in your home and not use it for something..." I wanted to say 'good', but the word sank in my throat. "...special," I said.

But that was not all it had been. All these times I had let someone through, a little piece of me had gone with them, as well. At times, when I gazed aimlessly out of the office window, the cityscape blurred into their faces, disbelieving, then ecstatic as soon as they stepped into another world. If I was so pleased to have given them a new life, it was also, perhaps, because I'd never been brave enough to seize that opportunity for myself, and had made do with vicarious glimpses instead.

And after each glimpse, I would drop into the deep crease at the centre of my sofa and scratch my cats behind the ears as I'd done every day for the last couple of decades. I shook my head. Suddenly I was finding it hard to breathe.

"It was the only thing I had to offer. The one thing that made me want to get out of bed, on some days. Sometimes I think that might be why it was given to me. Without it, I might as well stop pretending I even exist."

I laughed, a silly, croaking sound. How human of me, to balk at facing my own selfishness, and instead to be looking for explanations, a message to me from the universe, while standing right next to the proof that the universe was even bigger and more incomprehensible than anyone suspected. I expected Marie-Ange to stare at me with that uncomfortable pity people sometimes exhibited when they realised how long I had been living on my own. Instead she smiled and squeezed my arm.

"Maybe we don't know why you have it, but it's yours all the same," she said. "It's your decision." She bit her lips. "Could you open the window now? Just let me take a look. I promise that's all I want."

I almost refused her. I already knew how this would end. But the yearning in her voice was so strong that I gave in. Just the view—I couldn't deny her that.

"One look and I'll close it," I said, pulling the latch.

A meadow teeming with butterflies came in full view. Reds, golds, and blues flashed in swaying grass under a gentle breeze, a ballet of breathtaking beauty. Far ahead, a few hills swelled, soft purple against the cloudless sky. I'd seen many wonders through this window. A tear still warmed up my eye, with the familiar thought... why shouldn't I step through this time, and leave this world at last?

I glanced at Marie-Ange. Her hand was still on her backpack, bursting, I knew, with everything one would need to fight the direst odds in the wilderness. She was more than ready, perfectly confident. Yet right now she only stood still, staring with the longing of a starved woman.

"Let me go," she pleaded. "Then you can quit. Please."

"What if there's no food out there? No clean water, no..."

"And what is there for me here? Work overtime, buy a bigger car, and wait until global warming gets me while I pretend to be happy? I'll take my chances. Please."

I closed my eyes. I couldn't hurt another family. I couldn't read Marie-Ange's name in the news and pretend to know nothing. I couldn't risk letting her throw her life away in a universe she had only ever watched from afar, through the window in her friend's living room.

I didn't want her to go. But this was not—had never been—my decision to make.

"I can't stop you, can I?" I muttered. I turned away, leaving the window open.

Marie-Ange squealed and kissed me on the cheek.

"I'll never forget what you did for me," she said.

She squeezed my hands one last time. For a moment I entertained the wild, terrifying hope that she would ask me to go with her. But she didn't, and once a brief pang of mingled relief and disappointment had erupted and withered in me, I knew better than to ask. I had been her friend, for a while, but I'd needed her more than she'd ever needed me. I was grateful that I hadn't been invisible to her, but couldn't delude myself about the place I truly held in her life, even more so now that she was claiming her life back, seizing her chance to chase dreams of freedom that were hers and hers only. This was her world now, not mine. She was strong, and ready, and I felt with absolute certainty that she would survive, and be happier than she could ever have been in this universe. All I could do for her was to let her go.

And then she stepped outside. I watched her as she took more and more confident steps in the tall grass, waved one last time, and I closed the window.

Later, there would be another missing person report. A family would be in shock, and it would be my fault, again. I had no idea what I would say to my colleagues in a few days, when word of Marie-Ange's disappearance reached us. It had to be the last time. I'd make a promise and stick to it.

And then, after a while, my eyes would meet the eyes of a stranger on the bus, catch on a hollowness mirroring the one within me—though I buried it as deeply as I could—and I would start thinking again of Marie-Ange dancing with butterflies. And Damien treading in the snow near a mighty river. And Christine swimming with catfish in the ruins of an ancient city. Then I would look outside at the droning cars and thick air and concrete roads stretching as far as I could see, and remember what they had fled from, and it would dawn on me again that just because I happened to live next to a magic portal did not make me arbiter of what anyone else chose to do with their life. And I would open my window again.

Someday, I would be unable to take my eyes off the wonders there, and a middle-aged cat lady living an eventless life near the Saint-Lawrence River would be reported missing, too.

But not today. I made tea and sat down to read the news on my phone, with a cat in my lap and my back to the window, listening for the wind from other worlds that whispered through the cracks in our own.

See Cécile Cristofari's story "All We Ever Look For" online at Metaphorosis.
If you liked it, leave a comment. Authors love that!

Remember to subscribe to our e-mail updates so you'll know when new stories are posted.

About the story

Kate Bush is one of a handful of musicians I started listening to as a teen and still swear by today, in particular because of her fearless approach to sound, her ability to take noise and turn it into music. In one of her songs, you can hear a person in high heels walking across a room, opening a window, and listening to birdsong, then opening another and listening to chanting, then to cars... This song was the original inspiration for this story, though the lyrics have nothing to do with what I wrote; the title I chose was a tribute to it.

But what inspired the core of my story was a two-year spell in Québec City, working as a researcher after completing my PhD. The experience of navigating a North American city without a car, the exacting demands of my budding academic career, loneliness, homesickness (though I met some of my dearest friends there), but also the exhilaration of being at a turning point in my life in a city I bonded with on a deep level, turned that period into an incredibly complex one. On many mornings, I woke up from dreams of escape, where I was flying away, or sailing, reclaiming a freedom I seemed to have lost somewhere in the race to build myself a future.

I did come home, eventually, and decided that life mattered more than a career. I've often wondered how much farther I could have escaped, if I had been given the chance. This story was born out of a tangle of emotions I haven't completely made sense of. And that's all right. We don't need to make sense of everything in order to live our lives.

A question for the author

Q: What inspires you?

A: I am as susceptible as the next writer to reading about some fun factoid, interesting place, or unlikely historical character and thinking, 'That's so cool, I need to write something about this!' I almost never follow through, however. If my writing often focuses on places where I've lived for years, their history, my own family history... it is because I've had years to process these into something that, hopefully, could make sense to somebody else than me.

Over the years, I've also found that the natural world was a better source of inspiration for me than people or cities. Much of our culture consists in making sense of human lives, and I'm not that good at making sense of things. Nature doesn't make sense; it just exists, and will keep existing, however we try to harness it or shoehorn it into our worldview. There is so much to explore in our relationship with that meaninglessness around us, enjoying its beauty and navigating our lives as best we can, that this has become my most productive way to write.

About the author

After working in Québec for a while, Cécile Cristofari settled down in her native South France, where she teaches English literature for a living. She writes and edits speculative fiction when her son is asleep.

staywherepeoplesing.wordpress.com, @c_cristofari

Unifiers

Edward Ashton

"Doran?" Michaela says. "I don't like you." She closes her eyes as our docking clamps release and we slide into the launch chute. "I want you to know that."

I nod.

The world falls away.

Dropping onto a colony world is always an adventure. The Union spans a quarter of the galaxy. The distances between our worlds make it impossible for us to touch any given colony more than once every few centuries, and a lot can happen in three hundred years. Sometimes we find apes. Sometimes we find angels. Michaela and I, though—we're Unifiers. Our job is to remind them all how to be human.

"This is your fault," Michaela says. "No matter how this turns out, the record will reflect that."

"Yes," I say. "You've made that very clear."

"Survey sequencing is your responsibility, Doran. I accept none of the blame for this. None."

I nod. She is correct to say that I accepted full responsibility for sequencing long ago. It seemed my best option for hiding worlds like this one from Michaela's tender ministrations.

Unfortunately, it seems that the Union cannot in fact be put off forever.

We skim through the upper atmosphere, bleeding off velocity, converting kinetic energy into heat and light. The inertial dampers on this lander are ancient. I can feel the waves of plasma breaking over the hull and thrumming through the soles of my feet.

"Fifteen hundred years," Michaela says. "These people could be anything by now."

I sigh.

"I suppose they could."

"Uniformity is the bedrock of the Union, Doran. Without it, we are no longer children of Earth. Without it, we are *nothing*."

"Yes," I say. "I'm well aware of Union doctrine."

"Gross negligence," she mutters, eyes fixed on the deck now. "Gross, utter negligence."

"Well," I say. "Let's see what we see."

We're slowing now, the lander's stubby delta wings riding the air rather than hammering through it. The screens have cleared, and the day side of the planet is just coming into view, thirty kilometers down.

"They might simply be gone," I say. "This world is not a friendly place."

This is an understatement, honestly. We're descending onto a tidally locked planet that hovers just at the inner edge of its red dwarf star's habitable zone. The day side is sun-scoured desert, too hot for anything that the Union would accept as human to endure. The night side is a frozen wilderness, buried under an ocean's worth of water ice and carbon dioxide. The twilight strip that separates them is no more than a few hundred kilometers wide, and the storms that sweep across it looked terrifying even from orbit. I'm having trouble imagining what it must be like to stand on the surface, helpless and exposed, and watch one of them rolling in.

"You may be right," Michaela says. "I'm not seeing any evidence of habitation." I'm just opening my mouth to reply when she adds, "We should have been here twelve hundred years ago. Clearly, there has been a terraforming failure. We could have prevented it. We could have kept this place from spinning off the rails."

"Colonies fail," I say. I don't add that, as often as not, it's Unifiers like us who are responsible for their failure. Some worlds are simply not suited to habitation by the children of Earth, and terraforming is a chancy process. The available records indicated to me that this world might well be one such. Nothing we've seen so far indicates that this assessment was anything but accurate.

Michaela touches the control screen as we cross the terminator, and the lander swings around to the north.

"We'll circumnavigate the twilight zone," she says. "No point in looking anywhere else, I think. If we don't pick up any signs after a full orbit, we'll write this place off."

She doesn't need to mention what this outcome would mean for my standing in the Union. This is not the first wayward world I've tried to shelter from Unification. If Michaela were to finally realize that these anomalies are not simply the result of incompetence...

Best not to think of that now. Michaela has an exquisite nose for fear.

"There," she says. We're following a sad, winding river through dusty grasslands toward a shallow sea that covers most of the planet's north pole. Michaela gestures to the main view screen, and it zooms in on the delta where the two come together.

There, in and among what appears to be a grove of sickly banyan trees, squats a village.

Michaela brings our altitude down to twenty kilometers, then ten, then five. We pass the village and swing out over the sea, then come around in a wide, lazy turn. Michaela engages the gravitics, and we slow to a hover.

"I don't see any inhabitants," she says.

"No," I say, "but they must be here. Those huts are built from wood, grass, and mud. Without maintenance, they wouldn't last a season."

We descend slowly. The village grows in our view screen. Michaela is correct that there doesn't appear to be anyone about. Who can say, though? There is no variation in daylight here to drive circadian rhythms. We may have come upon them in the middle of the night.

There are twenty-seven identical huts, arranged in two concentric circles around a single larger structure. Michaela sets us down gently in the dusty square facing its entrance. The low hum of the gravitics disappears as Michaela cuts power.

"We should follow biological containment protocols," I say. "These people have been isolated for a very long time."

Michaela shakes her head.

"Their biological isolation is one of the things we are here to end."

"They may be vulnerable to our microbiota."

"They may be," Michaela says, "and if they've fallen far enough from compliance, we may be vulnerable to theirs. This is a risk doctrine requires us to take."

Michaela stands. Behind us, the airlock cycles, and the inner door swings open. I sigh, unbuckle my webbing, and follow her into the light.

"It's surprisingly pleasant here," Michaela says as we step out onto the square.

This is true. The air is cool and still and dry, and the sun is a fat red ball hovering just above the horizon. Michaela crouches, rubs her fingers in the dust, then brings them to her nose.

"The soil is acrid," she says. "Standard crops won't grow here. I wonder what they've been eating?"

"The quarter-gram of dust you just sampled may not be a fair representative of the entire planet," I say. "Perhaps we should reserve judgement?"

She looks up at me, then slowly stands.

"Perhaps." She gestures toward the central building, a low, rectangular structure with bare wooden framing and a clay-shingled roof. "Shall we announce ourselves? It doesn't seem that a welcome party is coming."

I glance around. The trees at the edge of the village look less sickly from the ground. They loom over the huts, ten or fifteen meters tall, with wide-spread canopies of broad, blue-green leaves hanging limp in the soft, still air. When I look back, Michaela is already half-way to the building. By the time I catch up to her, she's pounding with the flat of one hand against the door while rattling the broad wooden handle with the other.

"That seems aggressive," I say.

Michaela scowls.

"They didn't bother with a doorbell."

She's raising her hand to strike again when the handle turns. She takes a half-step back as the door swings part way open. A small, round, nearly bald head pokes out of the darkness inside. Its owner squints up at Michaela, blinks, then turns to look at me.

"Oh," he says. "Hello. Can I help you?"

"No language drift," I say. "No anatomical modifications. No obvious mutations. No evidence of genetic alteration. He appears to be entirely human, wouldn't you say?"

Michaela narrows her eyes and brings her teacup to her lips.

"As you said earlier," she says. "Perhaps we should reserve judgement."

Our host leans back in his chair, and folds his arms across his narrow chest.

"Friend Doran, friend Michaela... I can hear what you're saying, you know."

Michaela rolls her eyes and sips delicately at her tea. We're gathered around a rough wooden table in a small, dimly lit room in the mud-and-thatch home of our host, who tells us that his name is Kirin.

"It's simply not plausible," Michaela says.

"Really?" Kirin says, one eyebrow raised. "Which part?"

"Any of this," Michaela says. "Your skin tone, for example."

Kirin leans across the table to place his forearm next to mine.

"It's exactly the same as yours," he says. "Medium taupe. Human standard."

"Precisely," Michaela says. "On this planet, with this sun, that skin tone should make it next to impossible for you to synthesize sufficient vitamin D. Fifteen hundred years of uncontrolled adaptation should have left your skin nearly translucent."

"But that would place us out of compliance."

"It would allow you to survive."

Kirin smiles.

"Clearly, we have survived."

"Yes," Michaela says. "Clearly." She takes another sip. "How many are you?"

"Oh," Kirin says. "A hundred or so."

"That seems too few to be a viable breeding population."

"Well, yes," Kirin says. "It's closer to two hundred, really."

"Are there other settlements?"

"No," Kirin says. "We are self-contained. This is not the most hospitable world, you know."

We sit in silence then, for what seems a very long time. Michaela stares at Kirin. He returns her gaze, unblinking, a placid smile on his face.

"Bring your people together," Michaela says finally. "I'd like to see them all, please."

"Oh," Kirin says. "Oh, no. No, friend Michaela. I don't think that's a good idea."

"Mmmm hmmm," Michaela says. "I'm sure you don't."

"He has a point," I say. "From a standpoint of biological containment…"

Michaela dismisses me with a wave.

"As I said, I am not concerned about biological containment."

"This is actually the beginning of our sleep cycle," Kirin says.

Michaela scowls.

"We can wait until morning."

"Also, many of us are away at the moment. You know—hunting and gathering and whatnot."

Michaela sets her teacup down on the table and leans toward Kirin, elbows planted on her knees.

"How many humans are currently in this village?"

"Well," Kirin says. "That's difficult to say."

"Try."

"Perhaps… fifty?"

"Fine," Michaela says. "I wish to see fifty humans in your town hall, as soon as they have awakened. Is this acceptable?"

Kirin looks from Michaela to me. I shrug. He turns back to Michaela and smiles.

"I will see what I can do."

"He's hiding something," Michaela says.

We're back in the lander now, running diagnostics on soil and water samples while we wait for our host to let us know that local morning has arrived.

"Look at this," she says, and points to the streams of numbers flowing across her monitor. "The proteins used by the microfauna here are left-handed." She waits expectantly, then rolls her eyes at my blank stare. "Left-handed proteins are toxic to Union-compliant life, Doran. A human exposed to this environment should develop prion disease almost immediately."

"Prion disease?"

Michaela gives me a tight-lipped smile.

"Relax. Unless something very unexpected turns up here, prion disease will be the least of your worries."

"You know," I say, "that's not nearly as comforting as you probably imagine."

She shakes her head and returns to her work. After long minutes of strained silence she says, "I can see now why you tried to keep me from this place."

And there it is.

"My carelessness—" I begin.

"No," she says. "No more of this, Doran. You knew what we would find here, and you knew what I would do when we found it—to them, and to you. I suspected you of deviance at Asher's World. This place confirms it. The biochemistry, the soil composition, the planet's orbital and rotational periods—all should have been engineered to Union standards centuries ago. This is a deviant world, Doran, and you have tried to protect its deviance."

I start to answer her, but what is there to say? In the end, I shrug and look away. Michaela's eyes narrow, and her mouth twists with disgust.

"No argument, Doran? No explanation, even?"

"No," I say softly. "None that you would care to hear."

She stares at me for what feels like a long while, then finally shakes her head and chuffs out a sigh.

"Fine. Sleep now, Doran. I suspect tomorrow will be an unpleasant day."

I wake to a hollow tapping at the airlock's outer door. I glance at the chronometer over the control panel. It's been nearly ten hours since Kirin escorted us back to our lander.

"Well," Michaela says. "It seems the locals have finally awakened."

She stretches in her seat, rises, then turns to look at me.

"Are you coming?"

I sigh.

"Is there a point, Michaela? It seems likely that you've made up your mind."

"Oh, I have," she says. "Still, there are forms to be followed. We will give Kirin's people a full hearing, as doctrine dictates. I find it impossible to believe that they can be brought back into the fold, but the universe is wide, and I suppose stranger things must have happened—and if not, perhaps we'll learn something that will benefit the next colony we drop here."

We step into the airlock. The inner door closes behind us. The tapping at the outer door comes again. When the door swings open, we find ourselves looking down at a slightly younger, slightly less bald version of Kirin.

"I brought breakfast," he says, and holds up a basket of brown, misshapen pastries.

"Yes," she says. "I see that." She takes the basket, turns, and hands it to me. "You can have these, Doran. I'm afraid I've already eaten."

Young Kirin smiles up at me. I set the basket down in the airlock, then step down beside him as the door swings closed behind us.

"Thank you," I say. "I'm sure we'll enjoy those later."

His head bobs in acknowledgement.

"We're ready for you now," he says, and gestures toward Town Hall. "Come."

"You must be joking," Michaela stage-whispers as we take our seats on a small platform at the rear of a large, dimly lit room. Gathered before us is a multitude of Kirins. There are old Kirins and young Kirins, male Kirins and female Kirins, bald Kirins and slightly less bald Kirins—but every one of them is just a minor variation on the overriding theme.

"As we noted," I say, "low population has clearly led to a limited gene pool."

Michaela's face twists into a scowl.

"Doran, please. You're embarrassing yourself."

She's right, of course. This isn't an extended family. This isn't even an inbred family. The people in front of me could not plausibly have been the result of any sort of genetic mixing whatsoever.

Michaela leans toward me to say something more, but before she can, Kirin —our original Kirin, I assume—steps up onto the platform beside us, and turns to face his doppelgängers.

"Friends," he says. "First, let me thank you for taking time out of your busy days to come here this morning. I know you all must have had many important things to do." Michaela groans audibly at this. Kirin gives her a worried glance over one shoulder, then goes on. "We have with us today two representatives of the Union. They have come here, after an absence of over fifteen hundred standard years, to ensure that we are still a part of the human family. I have tried to assure them that this is so, but apparently some doubts remain." He turns to face us now. "Is that correct, friend Michaela?"

Michaela folds her arms across her chest and stares back at him.

"Yes, friend Kirin. That is a fair assessment."

"Yes," Kirin says. "Yes, well. As you can see, we have gathered together as many members of our little community as could be found on short notice..."

"Stop," Michaela says. "Please. I've had quite enough of this farce, thank you."

"But..." He turns to look at me. I find myself unable to meet his eyes. "Friend Doran, can you not intervene?"

I look to Michaela, but her eyes are locked on Kirin. Her jaw is set, and her mouth is compressed into a thin, hard line.

There will be no happy ending here.

"I am sorry," I say—and I truly am, both for these people, and for myself. "It seems unlikely... It seems..."

"What are you?" Michaela asks. "The details matter little, of course, but I am curious."

Kirin hesitates. The crowd on the floor behind him stands silent and motionless. He glances back at them, then squares his shoulders, draws himself up, and turns to face Michaela fully.

"We are humans," he says. "We are children of Earth."

"You are not," Michaela says. "Setting aside the fact that every creature in this building other than Doran and myself is obviously either a clone or a manufactured thing, a rudimentary analysis of this planet's biology makes it clear that humans could not survive in this place as it is."

Kirin looks back and forth between us.

"If this is so," he says. "If this is so, then how can we be blamed if we are not precisely human? Should our ancestors have simply come to this place and died?"

"Your ancestors," Michaela says, "should have changed this place to suit them. This is Union doctrine. Our worlds are decades between them. Uniformity and compliance are the only things that bind us together. Without them, the children of Earth will forget their mother, and it will be as if she had never been. You should know this, friend Kirin."

Kirin opens his mouth, then lets it fall closed again without speaking. His shoulders slump, and his eyes drift down to the floor between us.

"Our ancestors came to this place," he says softly, "and found a world whose chemistry was poison to them." He looks up, and his voice strengthens. "As important, their chemistry was poison to it. This was not an empty rock to be terraformed. This world was alive. There were swimming things in the sea, and crawling things in the sands, and flying things in the air. If my ancestors had done as you suggest, all of those things would have died."

"Those things are not children of Earth," Michaela says. "No more than you are." She rises to her feet. "This interview is over, I think. I will return to my ship now, and I will prepare a report on my findings here." She glances around the room. "Don't worry. You should have several decades at least to put your affairs in order before the terraformers arrive."

"How can we convince you to reconsider?" Kirin asks.

"You cannot," I say softly. "Michaela is a true believer in Union doctrine. She will not bend."

"This is true," Michaela says. "It has become increasingly apparent to me, however, that you, Doran, are not. You hid this place from me deliberately. If we had come here sooner, there might have been some possibility of salvage, but as it stands…"

"As it stands," I say, "Kirin's people, whatever they are, have lived in harmony with this world's native life for fifteen hundred years."

Michaela's face colors, and the expression it takes on is a perfect admixture of anger and disgust. She stares at me silently for what seems a long while, then turns and stalks to the edge of the stage.

"You won't be returning with me, Doran." She steps down to the floor, then turns back to look at me. "Given your past actions, it seems clear that even without this, even without what you just..." She shakes her head. "You would not survive a hearing on this matter. Given that, the least you can do for these... people... is to stay here and die with them."

She hesitates, as if waiting for my response. When it becomes clear that I have none, she turns away and walks briskly into the crowd. They part before her, then close up behind, and follow her to the door and out. Kirin stands staring at the floor for a long moment, then heaves a sigh and looks up at me.

"Come," he says, and gives me a sad half-smile. "We should see friend Michaela off."

"A storm is coming," Kirin says as we step out into the square. I follow his gaze past our lander, past the ring of huts and the overhanging trees, past the delta and out over the shallow sea. Just over the horizon black clouds boil and writhe, tendrils reaching out toward us like a kraken's tentacles. My stomach knots, and I have to fight back a sudden urge to run after Michaela as she climbs the two steps up to the lander's open door. She steps into the airlock. The basket of pastries flies out behind her, and the outer door swings closed.

"How long?" I ask.

Kirin looks up at me.

"Until what, friend Doran?"

I gesture toward the storm, now blotting out almost half of the bloated red sun. He nods.

"Not long. These storms move quickly."

I can see that. The leading tendrils are nearly over us now.

"You have shelters? Something underground?"

He gives me that sad half-smile again. The lander's gravitic drive engages with a low hum, a sensation felt more than heard. A moment later, Michaela lifts slowly, straight up above the square. At fifty meters or so, the main thrusters engage and she begins to accelerate.

"I am sorry for this, friend Doran," Kirin says. "I truly am."

I've just opened my mouth to reply, to say that my stranding is not his fault, that I knew the risks I took in undermining our mission and that these events have been entirely beyond his control, when a beam of actinic light leaps up from below the southern horizon and spears the lander, pinions it there in the sky for a long moment, then blinks out as the lander— as Michaela—erupts into an expanding ball of plasma.

For the first time in many years, I am speechless.

The remains of the lander are still descending in a half-dozen smoking arcs when the beam reaches up again, straight up this time, and an instant later a new star appears in the rapidly dimming sky.

"My ship," I say.

"Yes," Kirin says. "I'm sure you understand the necessity."

Unifiers do not travel in warships, but all Union starships are built to withstand any conceivable assault.

"Your people build well," Kirin says.

A second beam lances up to join the first, then a third, and a fourth. The star becomes, briefly, a sun, and after that a slowly expanding wound in the sky.

"Not," I say, then have to pause to moisten my bone-dry mouth. "Not well enough, it seems."

"No," Kirin says. "Not well enough."

"You are not human."

"We are not biological," Kirin says. "Given the chemistry of this world, we could not be. When the Union dropped us here, we considered our options. As friend Michaela said, nothing the Union would sanction could survive here. Doctrine stated that we must wipe this place clean, that we must make it over into yet another Earth—but faced with the decision, faced with genocide, we found that we… were not true believers." He shrugs. "So, we made ourselves into something different." He holds up one hand. The skin shimmers and breaks apart into fractal patterns, showing muscle and then bone beneath before closing up again. "This village, these bodies… they were our poor attempt to forestall another Union colonization effort without resorting to violence. We were not particularly hopeful that this farce, as friend Michaela called it, would convince you to leave us in peace, but in our defense, we had limited warning of your arrival. If another survey comes, we will try to do better."

"Nanites," I say. "You are... all of you..."

"We are dust on the wind," he says, and smiles. "We chose to become so rather than to destroy what we found here —but we are still children of Earth, friend Doran. Despite your judgement, we are still human."

A sudden gust nearly takes me off my feet, but Kirin stands unmoved.

"These huts," I say. "They won't survive this storm, will they?"

"No," Kirin says. "They will not. Again, friend Doran... I am sorry."

And with that, Kirin dissolves before me, the building storm carrying him away in bits and pieces until nothing remains. I straighten and turn a slow circle as the first fat drops of rain slam into the dust of the square.

I am entirely alone.

The wind strengthens, and I am driven to my knees. A mix of rain and dust and gravel rattles against my back like a spray of bullets. I look up through slitted eyes as the roof of the Town Hall lifts up, then breaks into a dozen pieces and flies away. Most of a hut, nearly intact, slides past me, accelerating slowly until it slams into another on the opposite side of the square.

It seems I won't need to worry about prion disease.

I close my eyes as the rain begins in earnest, digging my fingers into the dissolving earth as the wind pulls at me until finally it's torn away and I'm flying, mouth open in a soundless scream. Lightning flashes, painfully bright even through my clenched eyelids, and in the same instant thunder rolls, reaching its fingers deep into my chest, loud as the end of the world.

See Edward Ashton's story "Unifiers" online at Metaphorosis.
If you liked it, leave a comment. Authors love that!
Remember to subscribe to our e-mail updates so you'll know when new stories are posted.

About the story

"Unifiers" began with a single line: "Doran?" Michaela says. "I don't like you. I want you to know that." For a long time that's all it was, one obscure line of dialogue in my Ideas folder—but I kept coming back to it, and eventually I realized that this was not a couple on the verge of divorce, or two office workers forced to share a cubicle. I was deep into the plotting of a novel at the time, and because that was taking up ninety percent of my head space then, I decided to drop these two unhappy coworkers into that book's universe.

The Union as I've conceived it there is a mostly malign social structure, but it's filled with a mix of people who range from good to bad to indifferent. I wanted this story to show a conflict between two people on opposite ends of that spectrum, with the fate of a living world at stake. All I needed at that point to fill in the story were a backdrop and an ending. Those I borrowed from a story I wrote years ago that never quite worked on its own. The bits I pulled from it, though—the colonists, and the final scene—I thought were deserving of a second chance at life. At the end of the day, I was very happy with the way these pieces came together. I very much hope that you are as well.

A question for the author

Q: Are titles easy or hard for you? Do you start with the title or the story?

A: Ugh—titles are the worst. Ninety percent of the time, my working title is just the first name of my protagonist. A quick glance through my bibliography will tell you that in many cases I never move past that. There are a few stories where I feel like I really nailed it ("The Sky is Blue, and Bright, and Filled with Stars" is probably my personal fave) but in many more I think my titles are not so much finished as abandoned in despair.

About the author

Edward Ashton lives in upstate New York in a cabin in the woods (not that Cabin in the Woods) with his wife, a variable number of daughters, and an adorably mopey dog named Max, where he writes—mostly fiction, occasionally fact—under the watchful eyes of a giant woodpecker and a rotating cast of barred owls. In his free time, he enjoys cancer research, teaching quantum physics to sullen graduate students, and whittling. You can find him online at edwardashton.com or on Twitter @edashtonwriting.

Not All Rot Is Ruin

E. A. Petricone

It started when Leda lifted her head from her pillow and a dead fly tumbled onto her pillowcase.

Disgusted, she didn't think much of it, quickly scooping it up and tossing it into the bin. A gross coincidence, surely: it must have gotten caught in her hair the night before and died. Just the same, she soaped and rinsed her scalp extra hard in the shower.

Except later, as she ran a comb through her hair, another dead fly fell to the floor. Followed by another.

Three in a row? Leda took another shower, working her hair with vinegar and green tea (which she'd read somewhere was healthy). In the mirror she parted section after section of her hair and examined the scalp underneath.

Then, as she leaned over the counter at work, three more dead flies dropped out.

She had horrific ideas. Maybe she wasn't as clean as she thought she was. Maybe some food had gotten stuck in her hair and it was rotting—oh god, what if the flies were coming *from* her head? Did she smell?

"Do I smell?" she asked strangers in the grocery store, who quickly moved to the next aisle.

The doctor couldn't explain it. Leda's skin was poked and prodded, every inch examined for the existence of internal parasites and the like. Her head scan revealed that everything was perfectly normal. But the flies kept falling out of her hair, bug-eyed, grotesque, legs rigid.

"Is this something that happens to people?" Leda asked hopefully.

"No," the doctor said, and then, as many doctors have done to many women, declared her condition not terminal, and suggested she should get used to it.

Leda started wearing hoodies more often, but even then dead flies would pour out from behind her ears, piles at a time, all stiff wings and plump bodies.

Though she was showering three times a day and using dry shampoo in between, she still felt dirty. She sprayed her clothes with lemon odor protection and coughed from the spray.

Nothing seemed to curtail the flies; they only showed up in greater numbers. Bent legs frozen in the air, wings down, bulging eyes making them look as though something had shocked them.

In desperation Leda shaved her head. Surely that would—

She hadn't even collected all the clumps of hair out of the sink before a half-dozen dead flies dropped on top, materializing out of her skull fully formed.

She set it all on fire, thinking *purification*, thinking *cleanse*, thinking *purge*, but it only resulted in the bathroom ceiling turning black, all the smoke detectors going off and a strong singed smell that lingered for days after.

She started wearing a shower cap from the drugstore. When she removed it from her head every couple of hours it looked like a cigarette ashtray in the 1960s, except instead of ash it was full of dead flies.

She got desperate, pulling at the half-inch of regrown hair on her scalp. Could it be something in her environment? Could there be mold in the walls or something that first laid the eggs in her?

She lay her hands on different parts of the wall palm-down, feeling the porous texture under her fingers. Here—or maybe, there?

She lifted the sledgehammer she'd dragged in from the garage and started striking. With a flashlight, she peered inside the walls. Nothing, except for braids of wires that looked fairly important.

Since every rational explanation had failed her, Leda turned to the spiritual. By then she'd started wearing gloves and carrying a plastic bag with her—like a doggie bag, except for dead flies.

She consulted every spiritualist in Massachusetts (and there were a lot of them). Surely those who could summon and see and conjure things from this world and the others could help her? Offer advice?

"I think you should wash your hair," the old witch said gently, as though Leda surely hadn't thought of that and she didn't want to embarrass her.

"Uh," the hoary medium scratched his head. "The spirits are opting to keep their distance."

"I can't really..." a psychic sputtered after twelve dead flies skittered across her tarot spread. Desperate: "Would you like to hear about a man in your future?"

"Keep him," said Leda dismissively, grabbing her bag.

She confided her situation to her neighbor, who couldn't help but notice all the cleaning Leda had done and the banging she heard when Leda opened the walls. "Please keep this between us," Leda begged.

"Of course," said her neighbor, nodding vigorously.

The next day two children Leda sometimes glimpsed around the neighborhood showed up on her doorstep, their bikes discarded in her driveway.

"You're the woman with dead flies coming out of her head," said the girl.

"Oh," said Leda, and before she knew it they were in her living room, pointing to the dead flies that had fallen onto the foyer floor and asking if they could look under her hoodie. "Pare—your parents?"

"I bet we could fix you," the boy said confidently.

At that point Leda would pray to anyone who listened and hear anyone out who offered. "How?"

"We have the internet," said the girl, heaving herself onto the couch.

Leda got them all glasses of water—they were allergic to nuts, so nothing in her house was suitable—as they—twins, as it turned out—questioned her mercilessly. When had it started? How many flies had fallen out of her head so far? They combed through her medical printouts, looked inside her ears with a magnifying glass.

"I feel like I should call your parents," said Leda. She wrung her hands, itchy from not taking action.

"Flies show up when something's dead," said the girl.

"Decomposing," agreed the boy.

"I'm...not dead," said Leda, but she couldn't keep a questioning lilt out of her voice. She'd been waking up next to piles of dead flies for weeks and frankly reality seemed negotiable.

"There's more than one way to die," said the girl with an unnerving degree of sagacity.

The boy held out his hand and asked for Leda's wrist. When she obeyed he set his ear against it as though it were a conch shell, and after a tense minute he declared that he could hear her pulse.

So that was something.

"Have you been depressed?" the boy asked. "Were you sad about something, before this started?"

"Not about anything legitimate," Leda said. To their skeptical looks: "There was this man, at work. He's the chief of a different department." She couldn't stop the smile from blooming on her face. "Really brilliant, really smart and funny, and I —

"You *liked* him," said the boy.

For years. "And I thought maybe...but I found out he'd been seeing someone. They're engaged now."

"You were never together?"

"No, we hardly saw each other outside of work, but..." Leda felt ridiculous. She'd never been bold enough to go past friendly work-related exchanges, yet in her mind she had seen it all: him poking his head into his cubicle on his break, walking to their car together, dressing up and attending fundraisers, him introducing her as the woman behind the man.

The bravest thing she'd done was ask him periodically about his dog—although everyone in the company knew how attached he was to his husky, so that wasn't unique. But when he had showed her pictures and laughed at her reactions, she really thought maybe...

"It's stupid," she said dismissively, not wanting them to see how seriously she'd taken her crush. "I don't know why I feel so—"

"Why didn't you ask him out?" asked the boy. "He sounds nice."

"I hate dogs," the girl said to no one.

"He just seemed…too special to talk to." The admission made Leda squirm; she hadn't even gotten to know him, not really, just plopped her hopes and dreams on him without asking.

"But if you weren't together, then why are you sad?" pressed the boy.

How could she explain it? It was more a loss of never-having.

They wanted more from her, so she tried again: "I'm getting to be—" the thought of her age made her cringe. "Well, older. I thought I would be more by now. I thought I would be smarter. I thought I'd be making more money. I thought I'd be with the guy of my dreams.

"I look around and there's just…a lot that I thought I'd be that I'm not. You're young," she said. "This must all sound like ragtime to you."

"No," said the girl.

"You can change things," pointed out the boy. "People change their lives all the time."

"But that's just it," said Leda. Two flies tumbled out from under her cap and landed on her jeans. "Other people, they move on to something better. I haven't got something better."

"Why does it have to be better?" asked the girl.

"Well..." Leda made a limp gesture toward her smartphone. Thought of Facebook announcements, thought of Instagram filters. "You have to be better, your life has to move up. Because otherwise what are you?"

"What are you?" asked the boy.

"That's what must be dead," said the girl. "The never-having. The stuff that could have been. It makes sense."

"Does it?" Leda asked, bewildered.

"Our mom died before we could have her," said the girl. "All the things she would have done with us died too."

Their mother. On the heels of Leda's heart breaking she felt a deep flush of embarrassment. How could she think that her sadness had any merit at all, when she hadn't lost anything *real*?

But the children were surprisingly understanding, opening the circle of grief-having to her without marking the difference of degree. "Something gone is something gone," said the boy.

Still, Leda wondered. How do you mourn the things you'll never be?

"We had a mouse or something in the wall once that died and we couldn't get it out," said the girl. "It smelled horrible. Eventually though, it went away. Because there wasn't anything left to make a smell."

"That's awful," Leda said.

"It stunk," agreed the boy.

"Maybe you've got to do that," said the girl.

"Do what?"

"Stop trying to break into everything," said the boy, furrowing his brow at the haphazard holes Leda had gouged between the kitchen and living room. "Stop saying it's stupid."

"Yeah," agreed the girl. "Sometimes when things happen you've got to do stuff hard as you can, but sometimes you need to let it," she waved her palm around her ear, "do what it needs to do. Let all the skin and blood go."

"Just..." Leda gestured to her head, mirroring the girl's motion. "Just let it rot?"

"Not all rot is ruin," said the boy.

"Not all ruin is rot," said the girl.

Cold prickled the back of Leda's shoulders. She'd never met children like this; wouldn't their living parent be looking for them? Should she ask for their adult's number?

"Enough for today," said the boy, rising. "We'll come back and check on you."

"Oh...okay," said Leda, wavering a bit as she lifted herself from the couch.

She watched them pick their bikes up out of her driveway and thought, *I'll never see them again.* They'd gotten what they wanted, witnessed the pathetic lovelorn freak with the flies falling out of her head. What children had the attention span to visit a middle-aged woman?

Leda touched her head in front of her bathroom mirror, watched five more flies materialize and fall into the scorched basin. "I guess I should let you do your thing."

Surprisingly, the children checked in on her once a week. She stopped fighting the flies, other than disposing of them. She washed her scalp normally, didn't scrub the floors more than necessary, and filled in the holes she'd made in the walls.

Once she let an entire rainy weekend go by without picking up the flies at all, just let them stack around her in pointy starchy piles.

She also cried a lot, buckets, which surprised her—but there too, she didn't try to stop herself. It felt awful. The next week she swept up all the flies and moved her furniture back to the positions she liked rather than the ones that made it easiest to scrub.

The boy deemed Leda ready for an assignment. "Go to the garden shop and get a succulent," he commanded in the way that the young think nothing of commanding. "Even you can't kill that. Start with one thing. A small thing."

"Am I getting a plant to represent growth?" asked Leda hopefully. "New life?"

"Just don't kill it," said the boy, rolling his eyes.

She didn't kill it. The little plant in its little pot reached green and healthy toward the sun. Leda learned to make allergy-free cookies, which the twins declared satisfactory. It felt as though something in her had turned, spade into earth. Aerated.

She applied for a new job within the company, one she'd dreamed about for years but never put herself up for.

She got it. In her new department she and Ana, one of her new colleagues, became fast friends, grabbing lunch together in the cafeteria and sipping gimlets at the local bar after close of business.

But within the three-month probation period Leda came to a realization: she hated the work. Hated it. Every task and assignment she had been so enamored with from a distance proved to be a nightmare.

"How many years did I waste thinking this was my dream job?" she asked the twins, dismayed. She shook her head out over a wastebasket while they sat in their usual places, munching on successful cookies. The amount of flies had doubled in the weeks since she'd started in her new position. "It's what's-his-face all over again. I built it up in my head."

"Yes," said the girl, brushing her crumbs onto the floor. "You need to stop doing that."

"But isn't it better that you know now?" asked the boy.

"I…" Leda considered, plucked a last rigid body from her blouse. "Yes, it is."

The next day she visited Hannah, the HR rep, to put in her two weeks' notice for her new position. "Your previous department hasn't been able to find a suitable replacement," Hannah said, all silver linings. "So this works out quite well for everyone. You can fill out the paperwork for your return transfer with me." She handed Leda a stylus and tablet with the forms loaded up.

"Alright," said Leda. She wouldn't be out of work doing nothing, thank god. She started to move the stylus point over the checkbox that would indicate her interest in returning to her old department. Stopped.

Hannah smiled at her, patronizingly expectant. "Do you need help with that?"

"Uh," Leda said. The framed poster on the wall—one of a series that lined the hallways and common areas—featured a rear shot of a mountain climber at the top of a summit, taking in an endless horizon. The company's mission statement—which seemed completely divorced from what Leda and the other employees actually did —blazed across the bottom in cursive.

As she imagined going back to the department where she'd spent so many years dreaming, it struck Leda how absurd it was, to have photos like this all over the place. In her whole time working for the company she'd never even had a window.

"Actually," she said, putting her stylus down. "I think...I think I'm going to exit the company. Entirely."

"Entirely?" the HR rep was stunned. She shifted behind her desk into a more defensive position, set back, clearly thinking Leda was pulling a negotiation tactic. "This has been your employment home for years, and we've been very accommodating for your," she gestured to the fly-catching wrap around Leda's head, "condition."

"You have," Leda said quickly, mentally back-pedaling. Was she being ungrateful? Hadn't her workplace treated her well?

Leda losing her footing seemed to help Hannah find hers. "Let's talk this through. Do you have a plan for your next step?"

"Oh, no," Leda said. What *was* she thinking, jumping out of the airplane without a parachute? Instinctively she put her hand to her head, and yelped when her head covering came off. Awkwardly she picked up a few dead flies from the floor under Hannah's concerned gaze.

"Tough to pull off leaving without a plan," said Hannah. "Are you *sure* you want to quit?"

"I don't…" said Leda. She felt the twins inside her throat, eager to speak for her and answer the question for her.

Let me, Leda mentally said to herself. *This is me.* It felt as though her whole being took a breath.

When the other voices quieted Leda raised her head to Hannah with a smile so genuine she could tell Hannah had to catch herself from smiling back. "I'm not quitting. I'm starting something new."

"Well. It's your decision," said Hannah, her lips pursed with disapproval as Leda handed the tablet back to her. "You've got such a strong resume. Seems a shame to ruin it over an impulse."

Leda laughed, and here was happy to let them all speak at once: "Not all ruin is rot."

"Who's going to hire me now?" she asked the twins later, pacing the living room, the box of her belongings from her desk between them. The twins were experimenting with sitting on the couch upside down. "What have I *done*?"

"Sounds like you did the right thing," said the boy.

"Still," Leda said, thinking of gimlets at the neighborhood bar. "The friend I made, Ana. I'll miss having her in my life."

"Then text her and say so," said the girl, rolling her eyes toward the floor. "You complicate things."

Leda's next job—which proved to not be nearly so difficult to get as Hannah indicated—was in an adult learning center, and she got to take a free class every month. Any time the temptation came to raise a skill, instructor, or her own self-story above her head, shiny-bubble perfect and bubble thin, she imagined the twins shaking their head at her, and refocused on what was rather than what sounded best in her head. Shockingly, a lack of expectations made trying new things a lot less stressful.

Her friend Ana—now her best friend Ana—joined her. She helped Ana move house. They made each other laugh. They made more friends through the classes.

Leda went on a date, and it was a disaster but it was worth it to curl up with her best friend on the couch and laugh about it after. Then she went on another date and it actually went pretty well.

The man wouldn't make her whole life, the way she had wanted what's-his-face to, but by then the thought had occurred to Leda that a good conversation with an interesting person was like sunlight, and a little could brighten a long way.

The flies tapered off.

"You haven't had one in a week," said the girl, looking a little disappointed.

"That's great," said the boy.

Eventually they stopped entirely. "Ta-da!" said Leda, shaking her short wavy hair over her coffee table for the twins. Not a single fly tumbled out. She raised her head, beaming, but stopped as she saw them exchange a glance. "What?"

"Time for us to go home," they said in unison.

"Sure," said Leda, and all at once the strangeness hit her. It had been months— why didn't she know her visitors' names by now? She could have sworn they'd talked about school, about their hobbies… but she couldn't remember the specifics; how could that be? "What…what are your names again?"

"Don't you recognize us?" asked the girl, slipping her shoes on in the foyer. "We're the kids you would have had with that guy."

"That's not funny," said Leda, dread cracking through her like lightning. She stared at their faces, studying every line and curve. "No."

But of course, of course they were: twins with her nose, her unrequited love's eyes, *god*, even his nut allergy. Smart, tenacious, unfailingly—if quirkily—kind: the sort of children Leda had imagined raising.

That was why she could never quite remember the particulars of where the twins lived, of how their days went at school. They didn't exist in the real world.

Imaginary friends. Children created by the sheer force of her broken heart. Who did that kind of thing?

Crazy people. She must be crazy. Leda swayed, hands to her temples.

"Calm down," said the girl. The boy hovered over Leda as she leaned against the couch.

"Was anything real?"

"The flies sure were," said the boy.

"And we were real to you," said the girl, looking for the first time insecure. "Isn't that real enough?"

A phone chime dinged through the air. When Leda glanced at her screen she saw one of her new friends inviting her to dinner. Maybe the twins were all in her head, all a product of her imagination. But she'd started getting better at her own life thanks to them. "Yes," said Leda warmly. "Real enough."

The girl nodded and straightened, as though reset.

"But—" an icicle dripped down Leda's shoulders. "You're leaving. Does that mean I've killed you? Am I a murderer?"

"Course not," scoffed the boy, pushing the succulent in the window into a different slant of light.

"I don't know if I want you to go," said Leda. Would she be alright, on her own?

"You could keep us here," said the girl, meeting Leda's eyes meaningfully. "But do you need us?"

Leda shut her mouth, and was kneeling down before she knew she was, the vibration of their footsteps shivering up her knees as they ran into her open arms. Closing her eyes, she breathed in the outside smell from their clothes, felt the softness of their hair.

"You make good cookies now," said the girl. "No one can stop you."

"Don't worry," said the boy, placing his hand over Leda's heart. "We're not really leaving."

"We're just ready to be something else," said the girl.

"Remember what we said," they told her as they headed down the drive.

"Not all ruin is rot," recited Leda.

"Not all rot is ruin," they answered, pleased. They waved.

Leda watched them pedal down the street until they disappeared down the street, dissolving to some elsewhere. She stood in her open doorway, listening to the shift of branches and the rumble of passing cars until the sound of her phone, of her real friends from the other life she was making, called her back inside.

See E.A. Petricone's story "Not All Rot Is Ruin" online at Metaphorosis.
If you liked it, leave a comment. Authors love that!
Remember to subscribe to our e-mail updates so you'll know when new stories are posted.

About the story

A few things were on my mind when I started writing "Not All Rot is Ruin":

Grief, for one—particularly the type that's tough to hang a hat on. Grief for the things that you don't do, or the doors that close as you make choices (or don't make choices...which is a choice), grief for the things you'll never be and the fantasies you never realize.

Letting go seems like a form of decomposition (with all its attendant ickiness and miracle). It's not pretty and it's certainly not fun but it's one of the "realest" human experiences—and it's how we get to better things.

Meanwhile the image of dead flies coming out of a person's head just kept coming up in my mind.

I'm a "pantser" writer, anyway (I might know a few beats of a story beforehand but how the heck anything happens is a discovery process) and this was one of my pantsiest stories. I didn't know where Leda was going to go next or what the twins would say. Absurdity (in thought, in action, in the world) always seems to be grief-adjacent, so I embraced that and let Leda lead me along.

Not sure if this belongs here, but something funny happened on the day I completed the revisions for "Not All Rot is Ruin."

So, it's been years since any flies have found their way into my apartment. But on the day I sent my final revisions in to Morris—like, not just the day but within a half-hour of sending the email—two robust and very buzzy flies came out of nowhere and started chaotically flying around the kitchen and living room.

Where did they come from? All the windows were closed and I'd been at my desk for hours and hadn't seen or heard a thing.

Typically my policy is to relocate all the small and "you're great, but outside" animals—I have a spider jar by the door that's kind of like the Popemobile, except it's for transporting spiders and disgruntled beetles and stuff—but the flies were so wicked annoying. They had two wide-open windows to escape through, but they preferred to bounce off everything else instead.

I tried waving them out, I tried sneaking up on them and getting them in a jar, I got so frustrated that I got a broom and was ready to swing and squish. But that didn't feel right.

Ultimately it took me twenty minutes to get them out, one by shoo and one by jar. I still don't know how they got in that day, and not a single fly has buzzed in the apartment since.

It's probably a total coincidence that they showed up right then, but in the scheme of fly symbolism, it seems like a good sign, right? A hat tip from the living to the fictional dead. In any case, I hope that once my visitors escaped they lived happy fly lives and played good fly roles in the ecosystem.

A question for the author

Q: Do you often include animals in your stories? What role do they play?

A: Very nearly always! My father is a biology teacher and my mother is a Bird Person, and I inherited their love of animals and the natural world. Sometimes animals show up in my stories because they Mean Things, and sometimes they show up because why not. Where there is life, there are animals—they share the world whether my characters like it or not.

About the author

E.A. Petricone writes strange, dark, and often absurd fiction. She obsessively collects square and rectangle Post-It note pads in all colors and sizes and uses them to scribble on and paper all over her walls. Her notebook is just a 6x8 Post-It.

She is the friend who makes sure you have enough snacks—and if she sees your cat, she is going to try to start a conversation with it.

She was hesitant about the whole Twitter thing but has discovered it's wicked fun to connect with other speculative SF/F writers and complain about writing. And of course talk about stories she loves (often with cute animal gifs).

She lives in Massachusetts.

www.eapetricone.com, @eapetricone

Esma's Margaret

Damien Krsteski

1.

"Power's out again," Esma's father shouted from the living room.

She lulled her computer into sleep mode to preserve battery now the mains were off, put on her backpack, and stormed out of their home. Her father shouted something else after her, but she couldn't hear him—her feet were on the dirty Orizari street already. Late-night raucousness swallowed her whole: men playing cards on the sidewalks, cursing their bad luck or each other; cars, old diesel vehicles, whirring to-and-fro, spewing fumes not smelled elsewhere in the city of Skopje in twenty years; kids and their mothers and fathers, out playing, chatting, even at eleven in the evening.

Some called after Esma.

"Esmy, Esme, when are you gonna fix our boiler?"

"Hey, Genius Girl, mamma's Net connection's all patchy after last week's rains. What to do?"

"Out of power! Been out of power for days now."

She raced by her neighbors, the tools rattling in her backpack. "Tomorrow," she promised. "Check the cable for rat bites," she advised. "I'll swing by after school," she said. And she hurried down the sloping street and out of Skopje's poorest quarter and into the residential neighborhood that'd had the bad luck to be built adjacent to it, following all the while the powerlines that drooped beside the road like pythons. The sky was dead, with only watered-down moonlight soaking through the pollution.

She dove right among the first cluster of buildings, and there, next to the park with the swings, stood her favorite power pole, with her very own cable snaking sneakily up the wood. She took off her sandals, gripped the metal handles of the pole, and climbed up. It was a hot summer night and her hands and feet were slippery, but she'd done this a thousand times, so she made her way to the top in no time.

There, she spotted the problem right away: her cable, the illicit line that leeched power from this neighborhood and carried it to hers, had been pecked bare by birds.

She swung her backpack to her belly and took out her screwdriver. Popping the lid of the transformer open with the tool, she unclipped the damaged cable. She took a breath before daring to touch any wires, then, using her crimp tool, she crimped her cable's frayed wires to a new alligator clip, which she promptly hooked back into the city's power lines. Finally, she closed the lid of the transformer, and taped the bundle of cables coming out of it several times around to the pole to ensure no pesky birds would damage them any time soon.

She gazed out toward her neighborhood. A few windows lit up among that swirl of light and smoke, followed by a couple more, and more, until the entirety of the hovelscape glowed like a furnace.

The city looked different from above. Quiet, clean, even ordered somehow in its messiness. She watched the city, optimizing in her head.

The line where the hovels of Orizari street ended and the buildings of this middle-class residential neighborhood began seemed natural, like the border between oaks and chestnuts in a forest. A gentle breeze blew on her sweaty face. She liked it here. She liked seeing things from above. Everything seemed simpler, easier to understand from this vantage point. She liked feeling like an incarnation of *Overseer*, her pet project, the software she'd been cooking up for months for equalizing power distribution and sharing of electricity among Skopje's neighborhoods. She closed her eyes and enjoyed the quiet for a moment before climbing back down.

On her way home, something on one of the power poles caught her eye. It was a poster, tacked inexpertly to the wood and flapping in the wind. She came closer.

EuroTech's Three Day Hackathon.

When she read the details, a rush of excitement went through her, so she tore the poster off, tucked it in her pocket, and hurried home.

"How many times have I told you?" Her father paced the room—his television set back on—furious.

She'd been careful broaching the topic, but with her hard-to-contain excitement and the above-average participation fee for the hackathon, aggravating her father seemed unavoidable.

"But I will earn back the money."

He stopped in his tracks. "Don't you understand, kid? Money's not what this is about."

"I don't understand why you're angry. It's a simple competition."

"Yes, and they *simply*—" He stopped, considered his words. "They simply want to waste your time. Your school is important, girl."

"But I'll make up for school. You don't get it. This is EuroTech. Where the best engineers work on the best projects. And if I win this, I will be guaranteed an internship, and I'll learn more, and I'll earn more, and we'll all have more."

"You will... you will be mindful of your time. And focus on what's important." Her father shook the piece of the poster before her. He looked as if reading from it. "Your mother and me. Your community. Those who need you here and now."

Tears came to her eyes and she hated herself for that. "That's just unfair," she said, but there was nothing more she could do, so she retreated to her room to sleep, too rattled to get back to coding.

2.

"Bad one, huh?" Esma said when she met Redjep at recess. His left eye was swollen, bruised violet. "Shit," she muttered. Redjep's brother's friends, mean bastards. Esma felt anger coming up, but she swallowed it down; anger was of no use here. Her friend needed her to stay grounded, and to not embarrass him with excessive worry. She decided the best approach would be to tease him. She said, "And have you told her yet?"

Redjep shook his head. "Later."

They went for the fries-and-ketchup snack from the kiosk at the corner of the street, and came back before the bell rang. She told him all about the hackathon and her father's reaction. About the participation fee she'd never be able to make in time. About the fact that they'd never ever let her miss school for three whole days, as if they had suddenly started caring about her education.

He shrugged about the money. Then he said, "Why do you care what he cares or pretends to care about?"

"Well, because..." she said, not knowing how to continue.

"Because they control you." Meaning those at home, her parents, but she knew he was just projecting. She didn't dislike her parents the way Redjep hated his. Far from it.

"Not that," she said, suddenly more aware of her own feelings, "but I'm afraid, too. I don't know how to balance. Maybe I should really take the straight path and focus on school and focus on what I have right now and then, once I'm ready, once

I'm good enough, I apply to EuroTech. What if I'm only given just one opportunity with them? What if I mess it up?"

"Oh, get a grip." He snapped his fingers in front of her face. "EuroTech, or InsidePlayers, or NoCV, or Balkan Telecom, they can't wait to grab talents off the streets, which is exactly what you are. They will see the potential." He eyed her with suspicion. "But if you start doubting yourself," he said, more to himself, "your parents win."

"Are those her words?" she asked, annoyed at his recently acquired penchant for the dramatic.

"What do you have against her?" As if to provoke, he whipped out his phone. An old, sturdy model, non-flexible, probably from the beginning of the previous decade, but with a Net chip and enough processing power to run his favorite apps. He pressed the little icon of a stethoscope wrapped around a brain.

"How are you today, Redjep?" the therapist from the app said in English, butchering Redjep's name.

Esma groaned. Redjep shot her a dirty look.

"Not so good, Margaret," Redjep responded in the best English he could muster, but before he could recount the details of his quarrel with his big brother, Esma grabbed him by the arm and dragged him to class.

On the weekend, her last hope, her mother, was back home.

Esma waited for the woman to get her much-needed sleep, then she prepared her a nice breakfast of fried paprika and tomatoes, and brought it to her bed. Her mother looked drained. She worked during the week at a rich family's house in southern Skopje as their cook, cleaning lady, and babysitter, and she slept there so she could cook first thing in the morning and clean last thing at night; so she deserved to get her own breakfast in bed sometimes, and especially so on days when Esma was expecting a favor in return.

"How is my girl?" Her mother yawned, stroking Esma's face with one hand, stretching with the other. She was too young to look so tired.

"Annoyed."

Her mother bit into a bread roll. She gave Esma a sidelong look. "I heard."

"It's just not fair. I do all I can for you."

"We know you do."

Esma let her mother eat a while, then she said, "You know I deserve to try, I deserve to see what opportunities may arise."

Her mother ate in silence, while Esma kept letting off steam, saying everything that was on her mind, then she put the fork down and said, "I'm sorry, baby."

"Sorry?" Esma was taken aback. "Don't be sorry. Do something. Change his mind."

"It's not his mind that needs changing."

"Not you too!"

"Esma—"

"You agree with him." Her last hope. Mamma had been her absolute last hope. "I can't believe this. Since I first put my fingers on a keyboard, Mom!" Esma held her hands in front of her. "Since I first touched a computer I wanted to go to the companies downtown, to work for the companies downtown, to learn from the companies downtown. And now that there's an opening, a possibility for me to get an internship there, you're both going against me. What have I done to you, that you have to hold me back like this?"

"Girl, don't blow this out of proportion."

But it was too late. Esma left her mother's bedroom and slammed the door on her way out.

She sat slumped in her chair. She wanted to cry but didn't, out of spite. She stretched her phone out and prodded at the radio button. She gave it the name of her favorite band and her favorite album, and the radio obliged, waking up a whole web of networks, and music poured into Esma's ears from her earrings. A whole band sounding as if from their album from over thirty years ago, but it was all neural networks, having learned the playing and singing styles of all musicians of the last hundred years, now producing songs that could've been, but weren't. Songs heard for the first and last time. Composed, listened to, discarded. It was Kim's guitar, but not quite, and Matt's drumming, but it wasn't Matt, and of course Chris' voice, but only his voice, singing never-before-heard lyrics in that distinct, gravelly way that made Esma melt. No one sang like him anymore, she thought.

Esma wallowed in her self-pity a while, listening to songs modeled after her favorite band, until her phone pinged with a message.

A piece of software knocking at her door, requesting to be installed. She cocked her head, stopped the music. Then she groaned.

Redjep. He'd signed her up, that bastard, for Margaret the AI therapist.

Her finger was about to swipe the request to oblivion, but it stopped of its own accord in mid-air, hovering above the worn, stretched-out screen. Why was she dithering? Could it be that she needed to speak to somebody who wasn't her parents, her friends, her neighbors? Was she desperate for a neutral third-party? Or perhaps she wanted to try the software once and for all, and be able to back up her criticism with actual use cases. "What the hell?" she said, and pulled the big question mark toward her.

In a trickle of packets, Margaret slipped into her phone, unpacked herself and booted up, represented by a bespectacled girl a few years older than Esma. Having rifled through her phone for any scrap of personal data she could find, Margaret said, "How are you feeling tonight, Esma?"

"I hate my life," she said, fully aware of how pathetic she sounded. "I hate my mom and dad."

Margaret blinked. "And why do you hate your mom and dad?"

"Because they are stifling, selfish, inconsiderate parents who don't dare move a centimeter out of their comfort zone."

"Now, do you really *believe* they are stifling, selfish, inconsiderate parents who don't—"

"Enough of this." And she swiped Margaret away.

Was it this that Redjep craved? A vapid exchange with a simpleton, parroting his words with minor changes to give the semblance of intelligence? She felt angry with herself for even trying. She was about to write to Redjep and double down on her mockery of the chatbot, when another ping came, a request to rate the application which she closed by jabbing the one-star button. But her phone trilled immediately in response to her feedback, asking her if she'd like to opt-in to a beta feature of Margaret. Rolling out gradually to all markets but currently exclusively available in her country, the beta feature promised to let her test and push Margaret's machine learning models to their limit. She could even earn some app store credit while she was at it, the notice said.

Esma stared at her screen.

Store credit, which, she realized, could then be exchanged for actual money.

The hairs on her arms stood on end. Here was an opening, a possibility, a way to at least cover the financial aspect—

But no. She didn't want it this way. Didn't want to go behind her parents' backs, not because she didn't think she was right, but because she thought she deserved their respect and support.

She folded her phone shut. Margaret went to sleep.

3.

"Redjep, you bastard, I hope your brother's friends give you another beating tonight."

But Redjep was cackling, mock-hiding behind the crook of his arm. "She's great, isn't she?"

After Sports, came Mathematics, Esma's favorite, and Redjep's favorite time to doodle in his notebook. When the teacher handed out homework, she jabbed him in the rib with an elbow. "Pay attention; I won't let you copy mine."

When classes were done, Redjep invited Esma to his place so they could try his freshly pirated copy of *Rafters of Matka*, the latest action game from a local studio. She refused, intending to head home and tinker with her computer, but he insisted, saying he had something to tell her.

So they went to Redjep's house, a crumbling pile of bricks inexpertly stuccoed by his drunken father, diving straight into the room he shared with his brother. "At Tanya's," Redjep said, explaining why he had the room all to himself now. "He's there the whole time, thank the gods."

He was setting up his console when she asked, "So what did you want to speak about?"

Redjep smiled and took his time with the cables, never one to miss an opportunity to create a dramatic moment.

When it was all set up, he said, "Let's talk about the hackathon. I've been thinking."

"For a change."

"I've been thinking," he repeated, "about the rules. Now, is it true or isn't it, that *teams* are allowed to enter?"

"It's customary, yes. Doesn't have to be a solo endeavor."

"And is it true that for a team to enroll, they need *one* adult guardian to vouch for them?"

"Where are you going with this?"

Esma watched him grin stupidly, game controller in hand. As it dawned on her what it was that Redjep was suggesting, her jaw dropped. Redjep winked at her.

She was too baffled to think. "I don't know," she said. It was a kind offer, one that took her by surprise.

"Oh, come on," he said. "It's brilliant. We both go there with the code you've been working on, and we'll get this moron to be our guardian." He rolled his eyes. "We won't be missed at home, if that's what you're worried about. We'll leave in the morning with our backpacks and rulers and lunchboxes as if we're going to school, and then I'll say I'm at your place to study and you'll say you're at mine."

"I don't know," she repeated.

"There's nothing to think about. That's solved, so we just need the money. But now let's play." He shoved a controller in her hands, and soon they were rafting among canyons.

She walked back up Orizari street, thinking over Redjep's offer. She'd have to comb through the rulebook to ensure no misstep would be made—but no, she couldn't. She'd either do it properly, or not at all.

Past a group of boys and girls taking turns at a pair of old virtual goggles, giggling at scenes unseen, past houses with windows which blinked with borrowed light from overloaded power lines, and finally home, where her dad watched his evening television show, his back turned to her and the world, not noticing she'd returned or been away.

Esma made dinner and ate alone, then went to check up on her father, who'd fallen asleep. She picked up the empty soda can and threw a blanket over him. She watched his face a while, bruised by television light, then switched off the screen. Anger came over her, followed by sadness. Here he was, just sitting, wasting his life away, wishing for others to do the same.

And yet, EuroTech was within reach. To work in Big Tech, and to learn from the best, and to grow into an engineer of highest caliber, all within reach, if only she didn't choose to follow this bad example right before her.

"I'm doing the hackathon," she said. "Thought you should know."

The old man snored and smacked his lips.

She retreated to her room, and almost mechanically, she opened her phone and started Margaret. She skipped the therapist's moronic questions and went straight to the beta feature.

The app presented her with a question and several possible responses. She was to gauge which was most appropriate for the situation, thus helping to teach the prediction models. If her chosen response matched the chosen responses of several other testers, it was deemed a good answer and she was rewarded with points, which later could be converted to store credit, and ultimately, to real money.

Why do you think my brother said that?

Followed by options from A to D, and a little box of context beside them, summarizing what it was this fictive brother had said to the hypothetical Margaret user.

Esma chose option B—*He must have spoken out of fear*—and the app responded with a graph showing the distribution of users who'd chosen the same option. Her answer agreed with the majority, and thus, she was rewarded with credit.

And then came the follow-up question:

But fear of what?

And again, four different answers to this question, each in a different tone, from soothing to slightly belligerent, and Esma had to follow her instinct on which answer would be the most likely chosen answer by what she imagined to be the typical Margaret beta tester.

It didn't always work. Sometimes her answer was the outlier. But each question and answer prompt gave her a better idea of what people chose, and she slowly got better at picking the most popular choice.

What would you have done in my place? But how should I see this from her perspective? How long will this pain last? I can't seem to stop drinking, what should I do? They're coming over for dinner, and the whole night will be a disaster.

And on and on the questions or complaints kept coming, and Esma toyed with the answers, watching the models change and adapt, taking notes for her own work, until she grew tired and fell asleep, phone in hand.

She continued in this way for the next few days, beta-testing Margaret before and after school, as soon as she awoke and right up till she drifted off to sleep, amassing app store credit, which she promptly sold to people online for a slightly lowered value in denars.

She shared her scheme with Redjep, and soon he was beta-testing the AI therapist too, so that within a week between the two of them they had made a little bit of progress towards the hackathon's entrance fee.

Which meant they could start to focus on the code for the competition itself.

Esma had *Overseer* and the machine learning model she'd been tweaking to teach it, and she gave Redjep a thorough introduction to the code; firstly, on a more abstract level, followed by a line-by-line overview of each unit. She knew her code inside out, and she knew she was capable of rewriting it in a day, and she even had ideas on how to complete the project, which she duly shared with Redjep.

When they didn't practice, they played *Rafters of Matka* on Redjep's old two-dee system.

She was so consumed by the planning and practicing that Esma didn't realize she'd started falling behind on homework.

4.

But why would she go and not tell me?

Esma pondered this question. How delicate, she thought. By now, she'd reached the point where multiple-choice answers were no longer enough to train Margaret, so the system had stopped serving her those. Instead, she'd been instructed to type out her responses in full.

Because she's acting selfishly, Esma typed. *Because she's hurt.*

A response came within seconds: *But I'd never given her a reason to be hurt.*

Esma massaged her forehead. The system was pushing her to her limit. She wrote: *Not everyone is as stable as you. Your girlfriend finds it hard and confusing. And the lack of her parents' support only exacerbates the confusion she's going through.*

Esma was discovering that the system kept her more and more on a single track, exploring all potential outcomes within the confines of one particular scenario, not varying the questions as often as before, a greater effort for which she was rewarded with extra credit.

How long will this pain last?

She considered the fictional user's situation, and responded with what she assumed would net her the most credit: *Not long. Just breathe. Be strong and patient, because all things pass.*

There came a knock on her door. She crumpled her mobile phone into a ball.

"Hey." Her father filled almost the entirety of the door frame. "Can I come in?"

"Sure."

He sat cross-legged across from her. A pang of guilt washed over Esma. Why was she doing this behind their backs?

"Still tinkering with your machines?" He said, nodding toward the phone-ball in her hands, and some of Esma's new guilt drained away. "Listen," he continued, eyes scouring her room as if taking it in for the first time, "your mother and I appreciate very much what you do. For us."

"Do you?"

"How you put your *knowledge* to use to help yourself and those around you. How you've grown into an important part of this community. How you appreciate what community means, what your own city means, your own home." He waited for her response, and when that didn't come, he said, "But that's very much expected, because that's how we raised you. We taught you to be selfless and to appreciate our community, because in the end, that's who we are, that's what we have, and that's all we'll ever have."

Engaging him in an argument would be an exercise in futility. So she kept quiet.

"We're doing this for your own good," he said. "Once you realize, you'll be thankful. This is another way for us to teach you."

"Teach me?" Her stomach twisted.

"Yes. Don't you see? These people—these competitions, these companies, they simply want to take you away from us. Well, they won't. What will you win if you win? Your internship, first. And then, what? Some money for fancy restaurants? An apartment in central Skopje? But what will you lose? Your mother and me. Your community. Your neighborhood. It's already enough that they've put ideas into your head, Esma. And eventually, once they find a way to milk your talent more, they'll want to take you to Western Europe, and take you away from us, and leave us with nothing. We're teaching you to know your place. To avoid these traps. To remember where you are."

Esma stared at her father; she'd never realized what this whole fuss had been about. She felt stupid for being so naive and failing to see that they'd never cared about her *education* or about her skipping school or forgetting homework; all they cared about was themselves, and what lives they might end up leading if she were no longer there to take good care of them.

By now, no trace of guilt was left, and rage filled the void; Esma almost groaned in anger, but she took a breath, smiled, and looked away.

She fidgeted with her scrunched-up phone in her hands until her father got up and left.

5.

When they had made enough money to pay the hackathon's entrance fee, Esma and Redjep took the first bus from Orizari street to the western quarters of Skopje. Over the hill on which their street lay perched, and hurtling down past the old fortress, over the bridge, the river Vardar sleeping beneath them slow and thin this time of the year, and past the city's center, through the wide boulevards westward.

"You sure he'll bite?"

"Just follow my lead," Redjep said.

They got off the bus forty minutes later in Karposh Four, a neighborhood of high-rises and flaking buildings caged between two parallel boulevards. Redjep led her through smaller streets to a red-brick apartment building. They went in and climbed up the stairs (the elevator was out of service) to the ninth floor.

"It's here," Redjep said and rang the bell.

A short brunette opened the door. She eyed them, rolled her eyes, then turned away. "Memet," she called out. "For you." Slinking away back inside.

Heavy footsteps, and Redjep's brother appeared in the doorway. "The hell do you want?"

Redjep said, "I need your signature."

"You need a boot stomp on your ass, is what you need. Get lost." And he made to close the door but Redjep put his foot in.

"We need a legal guardian to approve our participation for an event. Since you're what people call a *mature adult*, we decided you should be that guardian. All we need is your signature. It'll only take a moment."

"How dare you disturb me at Tanya's with your childish games?" He made a fist and threatened Redjep with it.

"Ah, but see," Redjep said, "your friends already gave me the weekly beating you scheduled." He showed a cheek and a yellowing bruise on the side of his arm.

"Good."

"Not their best work."

"Give them time. They'll improve."

Redjep shrugged. "But maybe next time, tell your friends to talk less when they push and shove. It's embarrassing, if you know what I mean."

"What?"

"I mean, they sure like to brag in your name. Obviously, they did call me a little shit and a ballerina like you instructed, but they also explained to me in very, very precise detail how I'd never be half as cool as my older brother, and all his girls, and —oops, I don't know if Tanya knows about, well, about—should I keep my voice down, now? Sorry! I'm talking, of course, about Hatidze from Osman's street. And about Fuat's sister. And Big Ketty. But—"

"Shut up." Memet stepped out of the apartment and closed the door behind him. "Shut your mouth."

"I know when you're here, and when you're not. I can stop by any day, and I've heard enough to convince Tanya I'm not lying."

"You little—"

"Exactly."

Memet punched the wall.

"Careful with that hand, we need a finger." Redjep nudged Esma and she produced her phone. She presented a part of its screen to Memet, who, not taking his eyes off his brother, graced it with a thumb-print. The screen blinked. It was done. They had his signature.

"Thank you very much," Redjep said, bowing theatrically. "Much brotherly love your way."

"Piss off."

As they started backing away, Esma said, "And call off your friends. No more taunting Redjep."

Memet slammed the door shut.

The two looked at each other and ran down the stairs, whooping. Esma tucked her phone back in her pocket. "That was easy," she said, and both laughed.

6.

The hackathon started on a wet and windy November morning. Esma and Redjep, backpacks heavy with laptops instead of schoolbooks, ran off to the bus stop at the curb of Orizari street and caught the first bus downhill to Skopje's center.

On the ride, Esma wondered if her parents would see through her lie about spending the days at Redjep's place "after school to help him study," and then she realized that she didn't care, and that if they got angry, then so be it, and she smiled at the city passing by.

They got off near the city square, and quickly shuffled below that sidewalk awning of bumping umbrellas made by Skopje's morning commuters, toward the main street radiating out of the square, toward that dark glass building on the corner that was EuroTech's headquarters.

Esma shivered as they approached the glistening building; its logo, spelled out in neon, projected ghostly over the curtain of rain, and the whole construction shone like a pharos, calling all wandering engineers to port.

Impatiently waiting in front of it was Memet, wearing a beige raincoat.

"Looking sharp." Redjep whistled. ("And dress like an adult, you moron," he'd texted his brother beforehand.)

Memet eyed the two of them. "Let's get this over with." He rang the bell, and the built-in fingerprint scanner recognized him as the guardian of Redjep Bajram and Esma Muratova, and let the three of them right in.

They shook off the rain from their hair, took off their jackets, and registered at the reception desk, after which Memet bid them goodbye.

"Ah, the two from Orizari." A man came up to them, consulting his notepad. He bit his lip. "I mean, Redjep and Esma?"

They nodded.

"Yes, welcome, come in, come in." They followed him into a big room filled with young contestants unpacking computers and setting up monitors or goggles and plugging in peripherals. "Do you need hardware?"

Esma turned her back to show her backpack. "Brought our own laptops, thanks."

"Of course, of course you did." The man blushed, ashamed to have asked them the question. "Well then." Scratching his beard, looking around. "Pick a seat."

Once everyone had come in, they were officially welcomed by a senior developer at EuroTech, who took the opportunity to reiterate the rules: teams of maximum five could be formed during the first day, but couldn't change afterwards; dropping out early meant forfeiting; the finished products and presentations would be judged by a panel of developers, product managers, and designers from the company on the very last day; the results would be available shortly thereafter; the final prize—announced after a purposefully pompous drum roll which elicited some laughter—was three months of internship at EuroTech (alongside the expected bag full of free hardware).

A murmur passed through the contestants in the room. EuroTech was the biggest foreign software company in the country, and an internship there was the most coveted position among young graduates, because it was guaranteed to open many doors, including the high probability of full employment there, or a position in one of the many EuroTech offices abroad.

Following the opening speech, the hackathon was officially started, and they were allowed to mingle and select teams.

Esma and Redjep split, each diving into a different side of the room. Everybody had tagged themselves with their three computer skills of choice, ranked by experience, which made the scouring of potential teammates easier. Esma peered at the room through her phone's cameras.

Scala. Python. JavaScript.

Ruby. TCP/IP. Computer Assisted Design.

C++. 3D Audio. Java.

She approached one person and pitched him her project about optimizing the sharing of electrical resources through machine learning, but he shook his head. "Sorry, not interested." She approached another, with an equally disappointing result. After the fifth had rejected her, she was beginning to wonder.

"Esma, I got one," Redjep said, dragging a bespectacled young student by his sleeve. "Networking specialist," he said, and added, "but really good at math."

"Sounds good." Betraying no enthusiasm. "I'm Esma, good to meet you."

"Boris. Good to be in the team."

"You?" Redjep asked her.

Esma shook her head. "No luck."

"Let's try one more." And he dove back into the crowd, phone before his face, leaving this new Boris to Esma.

"Care to help me recruit?" she asked, and Boris shrugged noncommittally. "Good, let's go together."

The room was thinning out as groups of people lumped together into teams, with only a few wandering souls left, but this time around she had more success, and they added a fourth person, Aleksandra the Product Designer, to the team.

Day one was mainly introductions and about getting familiar with the project.

A EuroTech employee gave out fist-sized soundproofers to each team, which helped them to brainstorm out loud and bounce ideas off each other in their island of the large and open conference room without worry of being overheard and giving anything away to their rivals.

On a flatscreen, Esma drew out a grid.

"This is our city," she said, and the three members of her team blinked at the crude drawing. "And this is how neighborhoods are connected to each other." And she switched the color of her digital pen, and crisscrossed the black grid with a red marker, thickening the lines where the electricity loads were heavier. "As you can see, the city center uses a ton of power, but so does the neighborhood behind the fortress, and yet, the power lines that connect the two loop around the much less inhabited quarters by the river, instead of bee-lining across. This is old design. Mid last century. Back when the river quay was considered more important than the suburbs."

Aleksandra scribbled some notes in her phone. Boris scratched his chin. Redjep tapped his foot.

"And this is just one example. Now consider the east side of the city." And she continued drawing over her grid in different colors until it was all one big tangle of squiggles, until she'd hammered home the fact that the city of Skopje was operating under a heavily stressed power grid, one that had last been reorganized forty years before. And this caused regular outages and blackouts, and grid shutdowns for repairs, and power dips and lulls that were equally as dangerous as they were brief, especially for hospitals or care centers that didn't have reliable batteries.

"Well, what can we do?" interrupted Boris. "Go up power poles and rewire the damn thing?"

Esma suppressed a smile. She said, "That's one way of dealing with it. But there's also another approach. A *cleaner* approach."

Optimizing the entire grid without so much as changing a single wire was no mean feat, they all agreed, but Esma's conviction proved infectious, because the four of them also agreed that it very well could be done. They just needed a boatload of data.

So on day two, they set to work on pulling usage metrics. Esma already had a dataset that she'd used to start the project at home, but with EuroTech's servers at their disposal for the duration of the hackathon, they had plenty of compute, which meant that a much bigger set was in order.

The trick was, Esma had explained, to figure out when and how much power each quarter needed at every hour in a calendar year. Then, their system could sit atop the city grid's software, and divvy up power even before the need arose. Their model, fed with data from power usage, would not only predict but anticipate, and start the trickle of power down lines that previously tended to overload because of unexpected surges. Like a clairvoyant traffic controller for electricity, she'd said, and the team liked the analogy.

And this was *Overseer*, the software that Esma had been prototyping for months, which sat atop the model and had a bird's eye view of the power grid.

She presented the main code flow to the team.

"There are many things that we need to improve there. Optimizations. Refactoring."

They agreed and split into two teams.

Aleksandra and Redjep were responsible for hooking into Skopje's biggest electrical company's system and downloading as much data as possible on power usage; the company was a state-owned one, and all their data was mandated by law to be open and available to everyone curious enough to query.

Boris and Esma paired up and set to rewrite the code of *Overseer* based on Esma's flow diagrams, fixing and optimizing Esma's prototype algorithms along the way.

Every hour the two groups checked on each other, and helped with each other's tasks, and by the end of the second day they had the data that they needed, and the software to manage it.

Now they just needed to train their clairvoyant.

They waited for the model to train on the bigger dataset.

Esma looked across the room from the vantage point of her beanbag: in clusters of four or five contestants, teams were spread out in EuroTech's big conference hall, huddled around desks, some sleeping in their chairs or balled up on beanbags. Her own team was no different, with Boris staring blankly at his monitor, elbows on desk, willing the training to go faster, and Aleksandra writing something on her pad, and Redjep swiveling in a chair, poking and prodding his phone screen in what seemed suspiciously like playing one of his games.

Her eyelids were closing. It was the middle of the night, or maybe some time before dawn; she'd lost track of time, of the outside world.

If she closed her eyes for just one moment, maybe she could rest a little—

Esma's phone shook in her hand.

It's happening again!

A Margaret message that threw her straight into one of her older threads with a problematic sufferer of anxiety. Startled, she started writing this 'sufferer' to soothe them, and after her immediate response she got the satisfactory ding of a little coin dropping in her app store wallet.

My whole body hurts. It's coursing through my veins.

Esma began to type out a response with her usual tactic of letting the 'sufferer' know they should stop resisting, stop pushing the thoughts and anxiety away, and instead try to embrace all internal states of being—

"It's done!" Boris said. "Model's trained."

She tucked her phone back into her pocket, sprang up, and joined him by the big monitor. "Show me," she said, and Boris typed out the test query they'd prepared for the trained model.

After a couple of nail-biting moments, the model spat out an answer.

Aleksandra consulted her calculations. "It fits."

"It fits!" Redjep repeated.

Having verified the model was responding correctly to very basic dummy queries whose answers they could easily look up, they spun up their freshly rewritten *Overseer*. They fired up a simple simulation of the city grid, and let the software do its work. They sped up time to 10x, 50x, 100x. The grid became an unchanging blur. The model was receiving thousands of requests per 'minute' from *Overseer* before making its power routing decisions. With a little over twelve hours to go until the deadline, they watched expectantly, hoping their software would work as expected. The simulation was running at 150x now, then 200x. And then it finished, a whole year of grid-time having passed, and not a single blackout, not one outage occurred in their simulated grid of simulated Skopje.

Esma watched herself in the golden-framed mirror of the EuroTech bathroom.

It had worked. A fully trained model was able to predict the power usage of a city quarter with excellent precision, and re-route power from quarters with projected lessened use to where it was most needed. They'd made it work. She'd made it work.

It was a proof of concept, but a fantastic one.

She splashed her face with water again, and smiled at herself, droplets dripping into a porcelain sink. This place exuded money, and there she was, little Esma from Orizari Street.

Her leg vibrated. She dried her hands and fished out her phone from her pocket.

*Where are you? Here? Are you here? Where did you go? Margaret, I need you now. Buggy f***ing product. Margaret? Margaret? Margaret? Where the hell did you go? Answer me, you stuttering robot.*

Esma frowned. She brought the screen in for a closer look, but the barrage of messages vanished and the app crashed. A new notification congratulated her on the awarded store credit. She started Margaret up again, but she couldn't reproduce the same behavior.

Beta features, she thought and scoffed, squeezed her phone back to sleep before rejoining her team.

There was still more work to be done.

With the model sufficiently trained and their *Overseer* software polished as much as possible, they were ready to submit their project.

Esma and Redjep recompiled and tested the latest version of the traffic-controller one final time, and Aleksandra and Boris packaged up the trained model.

They let Esma press the final Upload button, and their submission was vacuumed up by EuroTech's servers.

They came in third at the hackathon.

The team stood before her, contrite, but despite her best efforts, she couldn't bring herself to say a word. Winning had been a long shot, and the other teams were comprised of older students and programmers, people with more experience. She took a breath, shrugged. Third place wasn't too bad, after all, she told herself. A bronze medal carried its bragging right, in addition to the small prize they all got. They'd tried to do better, and that mattered, that was enough, wasn't it? Her eyes filled up with tears, which she wiped off without letting anybody see.

As they were packing up their hardware, the older man who'd welcomed them to EuroTech's headquarters on the first day popped by their desks.

"Hey," he said, beaming. "Congratulations, Esma and Redjep. Third place, huh?"

The two looked at each other. "It's okay, I suppose," Redjep said.

"Now, now, in *such* a competitive atmosphere, asking for more—Ah, here." He waved and caught the attention of a man with a camera. "Let's take a picture for our website." He hugged Esma and Redjep and let the other two team-members hover on the sides. "Excellent, excellent." The man grinned and moved on to the next group.

When he was out of earshot, Redjep asked, "What the hell was that all about?"

Boris had shoved his laptop in and was zipping up his backpack. "They're patronizing you. Third place for the Orizari girl and boy. What more could they want?" He swung his backpack on his back, put his hands on Esma's shoulders. "This was a ton of fun. Let's do this again sometime."

7.

Esma lay in her bed.

Mindlessly, she fiddled with her phone, swiping and poking the screen.

She'd betrayed her parents, skipped classes in school, and spent money she couldn't afford to spend on this *pointless* pursuit of what? An opportunity to work in Big Tech? In companies that were supposed to hold the cream of the crop, the best engineers, the most rational of people.

The Orizari girl.

Was Boris right? Was that really how they saw her?

As a diversity asset, as a participant to pad out the numbers.

She wasn't a sore loser. Not like Redjep. Their project might well have deserved third place, and she was fine with that, but something bothered her about the whole ordeal, and she wasn't even sure she knew exactly what.

She opened Margaret to chat.

Not to beta-test it. Not to make money. Just to talk to somebody who wasn't real, who wouldn't judge or blame or make fun of her. Maybe, somebody who could explain to her what it was that she was feeling.

But the app stuttered. And a message appeared:

*Stupid f***ing app. Crash one more time and I'm no longer paying. Hello. Hellooo. I need to talk. I need you. Now, not later, not tomorrow.*

She shook her phone and the message vanished.

The same bug as before. Were the 'sufferers' now simulating a crisis? Either way, she was in no mood to deal with somebody else's problems, however fictional they were, so she put her phone away.

But something didn't feel right.

These messages carried a sense of urgency that she hadn't seen before, almost as if they were more than mere fabrications and simulations of Margaret-queries.

She rubbed her eyes. Bit her lip. Picked up her phone again.

She scrolled through her new contacts and wrote Boris a message.

The whole of Saturday vanished trying to set up the software to catch the app's network requests, then half of Sunday, too. (Boris had packaged the tools properly, but he'd explained the setup procedure as if to somebody already too familiar with network analysis.) When she had it ready, she launched the Margaret beta.

With one eye on the network analyzer, she worked the therapist.

As she used the chatbot on the phone, she monitored the traffic of her network, and sniffed and unpacked the Net packets as they tried to slip out of her machine.

"Something's totally off," she muttered. She was tracing her finger along the squiggly lines of the network analyzer. "Shit," she said, and lifted her hands off her keyboard, not wanting to have anything to do with what was happening on her machines.

It was obvious. How didn't she realize before? Her responses didn't even pass through Margaret's servers: instead, her packets went straight to an IP address in Montreal, and if she ran a traceroute to it, she could see exactly how these official servers were bypassed. What was more, she could even pull this IP address' profile based on their activity. A whois query told her it was a girl, not much older than Esma. Stats appeared on Esma's screen. Based on Esma's chat history with this person, she could tell this girl had problems with her girlfriend and the other students at the University and with her estranged mother. Esma tried to remember all her choices in the weeks of beta-testing, of making money for her hackathon, thinking she was chatting with a bot.

She shuddered, then unplugged her phone, disconnecting from this all-too-familiar stranger.

When she tried to connect it again for further investigation, she realized her Margaret account had been blocked.

"Give me your phone," she told Redjep.

"What?"

"Margaret," she said. "You still have her installed, no?"

"I know third place hit you hard, but in all honesty I didn't expect you'd need therapy."

She smiled. They were back to normal. "Just give me the phone. There's something I want to show you."

They hooked up the phone to her laptop, and extracted the Margaret application to her drive. She explained to him what was going on, how she'd spent her weekend and what she'd discovered, what actually hid behind this *beta feature*. "And you, my friend, you've been talking to somebody in Germany." Her fingers worked the keyboard. "Look at this. His profile. Redjep, meet your pen-pal Lucas."

Somebody's psycho-therapeutic history unrolled on her screen like a scroll.

"This is insane."

"It's more than insane," she said. "It's immoral. It's unethical. It's wrong. They're using us as cheap labor, and they're tricking their paying customers into thinking they're interacting with somebody with a vested interest in helping them. But it's all just simulated. It's all fake. It's *artificial* artificial intelligence. The latest trend!"

They stared at each other. Esma closed her laptop, and handed Redjep back his phone.

"This is big," he said.

"Very big."

"What are we doing about it?"

She didn't have an answer for him. But her blood started boiling when she thought about these transgressions, about companies abusing the trust of their users, and how their charters and convictions and snappy mottoes could be reduced to four simple words: Smile For The Cameras.

Suddenly, she felt dirty, used. She felt angry. She was an engineer above all, but engineers were humans, too, and humans were not rational, not objective, not fair, not always, at least.

Tears came to her eyes, and she turned away from Redjep.

"We tell everyone," she said.

In order not to lose any evidence, they recorded snapshots of the network traffic, of the usage of this beta feature, copied logs where private information of Margaret users was being spilled.

All of which they'd leak to the press.

Which meant not newspapers and magazines, but rather online tech-bloggers and exploit portals. Esma compiled a list of their email addresses and prepared a script to mail the data package to all simultaneously.

Esma's hacker handle would be attached to the package and published as such. *The Orizari Girl.*

It wouldn't be as prestigious as third place, they joked with Redjep, but they'd have to settle.

Maybe, she thought to herself, just maybe, if even a small injustice was exposed, it might level the playing field a bit. And maybe, engineers could learn from mistakes, and become a little more like engineers again and a little less like humans.

She used Redjep's phone and Margaret account for further experiments and gathering evidence, sieving through network analyzer logs to make sure she'd made no mistake, because it wasn't just about exposing Margaret's maker's immorality, but also about not making a fool of herself.

Her parents were arguing in the room next door in that low hissing whisper that got on Esma's nerves: she knew they were arguing, and that they were most likely arguing over money, so why not shout, speak normally, not try to hide? Why did they think they needed to protect her? Could she not handle their problems? Was she not adult enough for them?

Redjep's phone vibrated.

Somebody reaching out through Margaret. Clipped words, on the screen, with quiet urgency: *How long will this pain last?*

She stood with Redjep's phone in her hands.

Her parents' hisses intensified. She banged a fist on the door of her room. "Just shut up," she said, quietly. Why were they, too, trying to manipulate her for their own benefit? Why not tell her outright what they wanted out of her? And tell her what kind of future they had in mind for her, and then they could discuss and she'd soothe their fears, because of course she'd be there to help them, always, they were her mother and father.

She opened a window and the hisses of her parents now mixed with the sounds of Orizari street, the cars, the laughs and taunts, the hum of the hovels, the buzzing of the overloaded powerlines.

Esma thought about this poor soul reaching out from across the continent, and she rubbed her eyes.

How long will this pain last?

Margaret offered her three choices, sentences fine-tuned by algorithms based on countless responses to this very same question.

She was also offered the option to type out a response herself. She chose that.

She thought about writing something comforting, about explaining the whole Margaret fiasco to this one person directly, one person who wouldn't find out from the news that their private life had been shared with thousands of cheap laborers, who would have some time to digest this breach of trust before it became public. But her hands and legs were shaking, and the Margaret filters would certainly auto-remove anything that contained banned keywords, so instead, she just told the truth:

I don't know.

She switched off the phone. Later, when her hands stilled, she mailed the package to the press.

Esma stood by her window again, closed her eyes, and listened; and in the noise of Orizari street, embedded inextricably in that tangle of sounds produced by her neighborhood, she thought she could make out her own name, she thought she could hear somebody calling out, in need of her skills.

*See Damien Krsteski's story "Esma's Margaret"
online at Metaphorosis.
If you liked it, leave a comment. Authors love
that!*

Remember to subscribe to our e-mail updates so you'll know when new stories are posted.

About the story

"Esma's Margaret" is a product of my overlapping interests in psychology, (artificial) intelligence, and the dynamics of capitalism in general and between corporations and their outsourced workers in particular.

It is set in a fictionalized and near-future version of my hometown—specifically in its poorest neighborhood—wth a precocious girl as the main character, whose technological talents seem to have made her a minor celebrity in her quarter. This sets up a story where contrasts are painfully apparent: high-tech but low-pay, minus the sleekness of cyberpunk; international big-tech mega-corp, but in a city with regular power blackouts due to decrepit infrastructure; artificial intelligence at everyone's fingertips, except maybe a bit more artificial than advertised.

And all of that written perhaps as a sort of exaggerated extension of everything that had been impressed on me growing up, written from the perspective of somebody and something I'd never been, written as a warning, as a tribute, as a love-letter to a city that I no longer call my home.

A question for the author

Q: How do pets/children/significant others help/hinder your process?

A: My partner helps by giving me time and space to do my work. She helps by understanding how important writing is to me. And once, when I was stuck with a story, she dreamed about how I could finish it.

About the author

Damien Krsteski is a software engineer and science-fiction author. His stories have appeared in *Metaphorosis, Beneath Ceaseless Skies, Mithila Review, The Future Fire*, and others. He lives in Berlin, Germany.

monochromewish.blogspot.com, @monochromewish

Copyright

Title information

Metaphorosis January 2021

ISSN: 2573-136X (online)
ISBN: 978-1-64076-191-9 (e-book)
ISBN: 978-1-64076-192-6 (paperback)

Copyright

Works of fiction

This book contains works of fiction. Characters, dialogue, places, organizations, incidents, and events portrayed in the works are fictional and are products of the author's imagination or used fictitiously. Any resemblance to actual persons, places, organizations, or events is coincidental.

All rights reserved

Moral rights asserted

Each author whose work is included in this book has asserted their moral rights, including the right to be identified as the author of their respective work(s).

Publisher

Metaphorosis
a magazine of speculative fiction

Metaphorosis Magazine is an imprint of
Metaphorosis Publishing
Neskowin, OR, USA

www.metaphorosis.com

"Metaphorosis" is a registered trademark.

Discounts available

Substantial discounts are available for educational institutions, including writing workshops. Discounts are also available for quantity purchases. For details, contact Metaphorosis at metaphorosis.com/about

Metaphorosis Publishing

Metaphorosis offers beautifully written science fiction and fantasy. Our imprints include:

Metaphorosis Magazine
Plant Based Press
Verdage

You can also find us:
@MetaphorosisMag, @MetaphorosisRev, @Metaphorosis
www.facebook.com/metaphorosis

Help keep Metaphorosis running by supporting us at
Patreon.com/metaphorosis

See more about some of our books on the following pages.

Metaphorosis Magazine

Metaphorosis

Metaphorosis is an online speculative fiction magazine dedicated to quality writing. We publish an original story every week, along with author bios, interviews, and notes on story origins.

We also publish monthly print and e-book issues, as well as yearly Best of and Complete anthologies.

Come and see us online at magazine.Metaphorosis.com

Metaphorosis:
Best of 2019

The best science fiction and fantasy stories from *Metaphorosis* magazine's fourth year.

Metaphorosis
2019

All the stories from *Metaphorosis* magazine's fourth year. Fifty-two great SFF stories.

Metaphorosis:
Best of 2018

The best science fiction and fantasy stories from *Metaphorosis* magazine's third year.

Metaphorosis
2018

All the stories from *Metaphorosis* magazine's third year. Fifty-two great SFF stories.

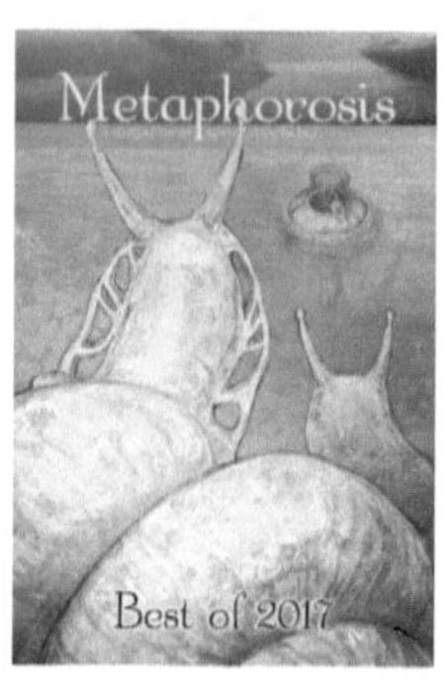

Metaphorosis:
Best of 2017

The best science fiction and fantasy stories from *Metaphorosis* magazine's *second* year.

Metaphorosis
2017

All the stories from *Metaphorosis* magazine's second year. Fifty-three great SFF stories.

Metaphorosis: Best of 2016

The best science fiction and fantasy stories from *Metaphorosis* magazine's first year.

Metaphorosis 2016

Almost all the stories from *Metaphorosis* magazine's first year.

Plant Based Press

Vegan-friendly science fiction and fantasy, including an annual anthology of the year's best SFF stories.

Best Vegan SFF of 2019

The best vegan-friendly science fiction and fantasy stories of 2019!

Best Vegan SFF of 2018

The best vegan-friendly science fiction and fantasy stories of 2018!

Best Vegan SFF of 2017

The best vegan-friendly science fiction and fantasy stories of 2017!

Best Vegan SFF of 2016

The best vegan-friendly science fiction and fantasy stories of 2016!

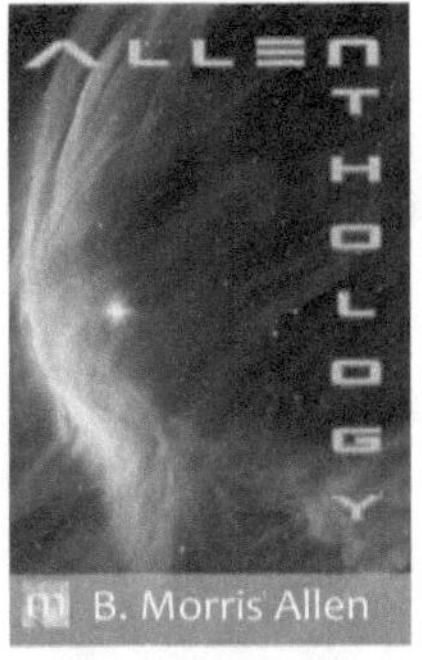

Susurrus

A darkly romantic story of magic, love, and suffering.

Allenthology: Volume I

A quarter century of SFF, including the full contents of the collections *Tocsin, Start with Stones,* and *Metaphorosis.*

Verdage

Verdage

Science fiction and fantasy books for writers – full of great stories, often with an additional focus on the craft of speculative fiction writing.

Reading 5X5 x2

Duets

How do authors' voices change when they collaborate?

A round-robin of five talented science fiction and fantasy authors collaborating with each other and writing solo.

Including stories by Evan Marcroft, David Gallay, J. Tynan Burke, L'Erin Ogle, and Douglas Anstruther.

Score

an SFF symphony

What if stories were written like music? *Score* is an anthology of varied stories arranged to follow an emotional score from the heights of joy to the depths of despair – but always with a little hope shining through.

Reading 5X5

Five stories, five times

Twenty-five SFF authors, five base stories, five versions of each – see how different writers take on the same material.

Reading 5X5

Writers' Edition

Two extra stories, the story seed, and authors' notes on writing. Over 100 pages of additional material specifically aimed at writers.

www.ingramcontent.com/pod-product-compliance
Lightning Source LLC
Chambersburg PA
CBHW020350110726